Harry Castlemon

Snowed Up

The sportsman's club in the mountains

Harry Castlemon

Snowed Up

The sportsman's club in the mountains

ISBN/EAN: 9783337255749

Printed in Europe, USA, Canada, Australia, Japan

Cover: Foto ©Andreas Hilbeck / pixelio.de

More available books at **www.hansebooks.com**

The Robbers Foiled.

FRANK NELSON SERIES.

SNOWED UP;

OR, THE

SPORTSMAN'S CLUB IN THE MOUNTAINS.

By HARRY CASTLEMON,

AUTHOR OF "THE GUNBOAT SERIES," "SPORTSMAN'S CLUB SERIES," "ROCKY MOUNTAIN SERIES," &C.

PHILADELPHIA:
PORTER & COATES.

CINCINNATI:
R. W. CARROLL & CO.

FAMOUS CASTLEMON BOOKS.

GUNBOAT SERIES. By HARRY CASTLEMON. Illustrated. 6 vols. 16mo. Cloth, extra, black and gold.

FRANK THE YOUNG NATURALIST. FRANK ON A GUNBOAT. FRANK IN THE WOODS. FRANK BEFORE VICKSBURG. FRANK ON THE LOWER MISSISSIPPI. FRANK ON THE PRAIRIE.

ROCKY MOUNTAIN SERIES. By HARRY CASTLEMON. Illustrated. 3 vols. 16mo. Cloth, extra, black and gold.

FRANK AMONG THE RANCHEROS.

FRANK AT DON CARLOS' RANCHO.

FRANK IN THE MOUNTAINS.

SPORTSMAN'S CLUB SERIES. By HARRY CASTLEMON. Illustrated. 3 vols. 16mo. Cloth, extra, black and gold.

THE SPORTSMAN'S CLUB IN THE SADDLE.

THE SPORTSMAN'S CLUB AFLOAT.

THE SPORTSMAN'S CLUB AMONG THE TRAPPERS.

GO-AHEAD SERIES. By HARRY CASTLEMON. Illustrated. 3 vols. 16mo. Cloth, extra, black and gold.

TOM NEWCOMBE. GO-AHEAD. NO MOSS.

FRANK NELSON SERIES. By HARRY CASTLEMON. Illustrated. 3 vols. 16mo. Cloth, extra, black and gold.

SNOWED UP. FRANK IN THE FORECASTLE. BOY TRADERS.

BOY TRAPPER SERIES. By HARRY CASTLEMON. Illustrated. 3 vols. 16mo. Cloth, extra, black and gold.

THE BURIED TREASURE; OR, OLD JORDAN'S HAUNT.

THE BOY TRAPPER; OR, HOW DAVE FILLED THE ORDER.

THE MAIL-CARRIER.

ROUGHING IT SERIES. By HARRY CASTLEMON. Illustrated. 16mo. Cloth, extra, black and gold.

GEORGE IN CAMP.

Other Volumes in Preparation.

CONTENTS.

 CONTENTS.

CHAPTER X.

CHAPTER XI.

CHAPTER XII.

CHAPTER XIII.

CHAPTER XIV.

CHAPTER XV.

CHAPTER XVI.

CHAPTER XVII.

CHAPTER XVIII.

SNOWED UP;

OR, THE

SPORTSMAN'S CLUB IN THE MOUNTAINS.

CHAPTER I.

A DISPUTE.

DID you ever hear tell of sich a thing afore, Zack?"

"I never did in all my born days—never! The idee of this little snipe comin' out here, fresh from the States, an' tellin' a man like me, what's done nothin' but guide wagon-trains acrosst the prairie fur the last ten years—the idee of his tellin' me that I am losin' the hul kit an' bilin' of you, an' that I am doin' it a purpose! I say it's ridikilis, an' I won't stand it. Here, Sile, hold my gun till I make him chaw them words of his'n!"

(7)

" You are very much mistaken in me, my friend," replied a calm voice, which contrasted strangely with the excited guide's insolent tones. " I may be fresh from the States, but I have seen more of prairie life than you seem to imagine. At any rate, I know enough about it to be sure that you are not on the road to the Fort."

This conversation took place one bright morning, between our old friend Archie Winters, and two rough looking frontiersmen, who answered to the names of Zack and Silas. The latter stood leaning on his rifle, and glaring down at the boy before him as if he meant to destroy him by the angry glances from his eyes, while Zack was rolling up his sleeves and making other demonstrations which showed a desire on his part to fight somebody. Close by Archie's side were his two inseparable companions, Fred Craven and Eugene Gaylord, who sat in their saddles, being mounted on the same horses they had ridden from Salt Lake City to Fort Bolton. Eugene held Archie's old horse by the bridle, while Archie's attention was about equally divided between the two trappers and a small bay steed, with black points and a white star in his forehead, to which he was clinging with both hands. The horse bore Archie's saddle strapped firmly on his back, and was kept in partial subjection by a raw-hide lasso, which was twisted tightly about his lower jaw, the ends being passed over the animal's neck and around the horn of the saddle to serve as a bridle. Like Roderick and King James, this horse had a history which shall be related in due time.

Around this group which we have described were gathered a dozen or more emigrants, men, women and children, who waited impatiently to hear what would be said next, and looked first at the guides and then at Archie, as if trying to discover something in their faces that would aid them in deciding between the disputants. A little distance away stood two wagons, the mules and oxen harnessed and yoked and ready to start; but there was a wide difference of opinion between Archie and the guides on a matter that was of vital importance to the emigrants, and they could not think of resuming their journey until it had been settled.

Having made his preparations for a pugilistic encounter, with as much care and deliberation as he would have exhibited had he been about to measure strength with a person of his own stature and weight, Zack once more addressed himself to Archie.

"We was all quiet an' peaceable like till you come," said he; "but since you dropped down amongst us all of a sudden, like you had come from the clouds, an' without nobody's askin' you to come, thar's been a rumpus goin' on the hul time."

"The rumpus, as you call it, was all raised by you," returned Archie. "You've had a good many remarks to make about us, but we have kept silent."

"Now you can jest toddle off about your business, if you've got any," continued Zack, "or take what follows. I haint agoin' to waste no time a waitin' on you, nuther."

"We have business," answered Archie, "but we

are in no great hurry to attend to it.   The prairie is as free to us as it is to you, and when we get tired of staying here, we're going to Fort Bolton."

" So be we," said Zack.

" How far do you call it from here?" asked Archie.

" A matter of thirty miles, mebbe."

" And which way?"

" Off thar," said Zack, extending his arm toward the north-west.

" Well, I say it is off *there*," replied Archie, pointing in just the opposite direction, "and distant about three days' journey.   I ought to know, for I have just come from there."

" What brought you so far away from the Fort?" asked one of the emigrants.

" As we told you last night, we have been following a drove of wild horses, trying to catch one of them."

" An' as *we* told you last night, that's a likely story," said Zack, glancing at Silas, who nodded assent. "You're purty lookin' fellers to ketch a wild hoss, haint you now !"

"Well, here's the horse, any how," returned Archie, jerking his thumb over his shoulder toward the animal he was holding. "If you don't believe he is wild, just put yourself within reach of his heels, if you dare. We followed the drove he was in for three days and more, and that's what brought us so far from the Fort."

"An' that's how you come to be teetotally turned round an' lost," added Zack. "You fellers can do as you like about it, but I tell you that if you foller them young cubs you'll never see Fort Bolton the longest day you live."

This last remark was called forth by a movement on the part of the emigrants, who, in response to a sign from one of their number, drew a little apart to hold a consultation. Their actions led Zack to mistrust that they were on the point of deciding against him, and this seemed to increase the feelings of animosity which, for some unaccountable reason, he had shown toward Archie and his friends ever since they first appeared in the emigrant camp.

"If they do go with you I'll allow they won't have much to foller," said Zack, in savage tones, "cause I'll wallop you till thar ain't nothing left of you."

"I don't see why you should want to do that," answered Archie. "These people are nothing to you, and it can make no difference to you whether they go your way or mine."

"Then what odds does it make to you?" demanded Silas.

"None whatever. They told us they wanted to go to Bolton, and as we were going right there we offered to show them the way."

"More like you want to show 'em the way to some place in the mountains whar you can rob 'em," snapped Zack.

"O, come now," returned Archie, "that's rather too far-fetched. I've seen whole families composed of such as you. There are some of them in irons now at the Fort."

"What do you mean by that?" demanded Zack.

"I mean that there are some men of your calling in irons now in Fort Bolton," repeated Archie, not in the least terrified by the expression of almost ungovernable fury which settled on the man's face. "That's what I mean. Have a care," he added, as Zack dashed his hat upon the ground with an angry exclamation and started fiercely toward him. "I have a friend here who will not see me imposed upon."

As Archie spoke he swung himself around beside the horse he was holding, which, believing no doubt that the boy was about to mount him, turned swiftly, thus presenting his heels toward the advancing guide, who halted very suddenly.

"He knows how to handle his feet," continued Archie, "and I believe he can kick your hat off your head the first time trying. Suppose you put it on and let him make the attempt."

Zack did not see fit to accept this proposition, and neither did he renew his hostile demonstrations. Whether it was because he did not think it quite safe to trust himself too close to the horse's heels, or for the reason that he did not like the looks of the sixteen-shooters which Eugene and Feather-weight promptly unslung from their backs, we have no means of knowing.   Perhaps it was because the emigrants had brought their consultation to an end, and having decided upon their course, came up to announce what it was.

"Are you sure you are right?" asked an old white-headed man, addressing himself to Archie.

"Yes, sir, as sure as I can be," was the reply. "We have taken pains to keep our bearings, and I am certain that if we have no bad luck, we shall be in Bolton in less than three days.   We shall travel as nearly south-east as we can to get there, too."

"Well, we have concluded to trust ourselves to you.   Bring on the wagons, boys."

"You'll never see the Fort," said Zack, whose rage was so great that he could scarcely make himself understood.

None of the emigrants made any reply.   The

women and children were assisted into the wagons,
and the drivers climbed to their seats and drove
after Eugene and Featherweight, who rode off over
the prairie. Archie had some difficulty in mounting
his steed, for the animal persisted in keeping his
head toward him, and it was only after repeated
efforts that the boy managed to seize the horn of
the saddle and swung himself upon the horse's
back. Even after he got there the animal did not
seem disposed to permit him to remain, for he
straightway began to kick and plunge furiously.
But Archie had not lived among the Rancheros of
California for nothing. By thrusting the long
rowels of his Mexican spurs through the hair-girth
with which his saddle was strapped to the horse's
back, he was able to keep a secure seat in spite of
the furious efforts made to dislodge him; and when
at last his nag was wearied with his fruitless
struggles, he urged him into a lope, and in a few
seconds drew up beside his friends at the head of
the wagon-train.

CHAPTER II.

WHAT ARCHIE KNEW ABOUT MONEY.

THE gray-headed man before spoken of, whom the boys had put down as the father of one of the two stalwart young men who were driving the wagons, was riding Archie's old horse, which Eugene had offered him, and was talking earnestly with Fred and his companion. It was plain that the subject of their conversation was either an exciting or an alarming one, for the old man's face was as white as a sheet, and his voice trembled when he addressed Archie.

" Do you think those men were wilfully misleading us, or that they were lost like ourselves ?" he asked.

" They certainly were not lost," answered Archie. " Men of their stamp don't get lost on the prairies."

2

"What object could they have had in view in taking us so far out of our way?"

"I am sure I do not know, unless they had reason to believe that there is something of value in your wagons."

"Did they mean to rob us?" cried the old man, in great alarm.

"Their actions were suspicious, to say the least," returned Archie, who did not care to say anything that would add to the old man's terror. "But you are safe from them now. If they come about your camp again, all you have to do is to order them away."

"I certainly have something of value with me," continued the emigrant, after a moment's pause, "and I am not afraid to trust you with the secret, for you look honest. There's a million dollars and more in that first wagon."

"Whew!" whistled Archie. "And did they know it?"

"They did, for I told them."

"Well, I wish you hadn't done it."

That was what Archie said aloud; but to himself he added: "You ought to have a guardian appointed for you, old as you are."

The emigrant said nothing after this. The knowledge that he had harbored robbers in his camp for the last three days made a deep impression on him, and he gradually fell back beside the wagons, where he seemed resolved to remain. He wanted to keep a sharp eye on his treasure.

"That is the most simple thing that a grown person was ever guilty of," said Archie, as soon as the old man was out of hearing. "Why couldn't he keep still? I'll tell you what's a fact, fellows," he added, after thinking a moment, "if there are any more men like Zack and Sile loose in this neighborhood, I'd rather be alone on the prairie than to stay with these wagons."

"Do you think we shall see them again?" inquired Eugene.

"Do you suppose that men like those will let so much money slip through their fingers if they can help it?" asked Archie, in reply.

"More than a million dollars," exclaimed Featherweight. "What shape is it in, I wonder?"

"If I had that amount of money, I'd travel in a little better style than he does," said Eugene. "He and his family are all in rags, and his mules and oxen look like the breaking up of a hard winter. He's an old miser."

"He may have an object in it," said Featherweight. "Perhaps he doesn't want any one to suspect that he is worth so much."

"Then why does he go and tell it?" demanded Eugene. "I wonder if it is in gold or silver!"

"Neither," said Archie.

"How do you know?"

"I just guess at it."

"But you must have something to go by in your guessing. I wonder how much a million dollars in gold would weigh!"

"If it was in eagles, it wouldn't fall very far short of thirty-five hundred pound, avoirdupois," said Archie.

"How much?" cried both the boys, opening their eyes wide with amazement.

Archie repeated his statement, adding:

"You know that such articles as gold, silver and precious stones are weighed by Troy weight. If you could put a hundred thousand gold eagles (that would be just a million dollars) on one side of a jeweller's scales, it would take a four thousand pound weight on the other to balance them."*

"Well, there's no such weight in that rickety old wagon," said Eugene, as soon as he had recovered from his surprise. "It wouldn't hold it up. It must be in greenbacks."

"How large an amount in greenbacks do you suppose you could carry?" asked Archie. "I

---

* There may be those who will be as surprised to read this as Fred and Eugene were to hear it. If they doubt the accuracy of Archie's statement, and will go to the trouble to make a calculation, taking as a basis the weight of a gold eagle, which is about 11 pwts. and 6 grs., and bearing in mind that a pound Troy contains 5760 grains and a pound avoirdupois 7000 grains, they will find that he spoke within bounds.

mean in small bills, ranging from ones up to twenties."

"O, I could carry all you could pile on me," said Fred, confidently, "two or three million, probably."

"Yes, and five or six million," said Eugene.

"That's much better than I can do," said Archie, with a laugh, "and while I was in the Fleet Paymaster's office during the war, I had more than one opportunity to try my hand at it. We used to get drafts from Washington on the sub-treasury in St. Louis, calling for two hundred thousand dollars. When the chief went up to draw the money I generally went with him, taking with me two large carpet-bags to bring the greenbacks home in. The money was put up in square packages of such size that two of them were all I could get into each carpet-bag. It was my business, after the money was drawn, to look out for it until we reached Cairo. In carrying it from the sub-treasury to the Planter's House, where we always stopped—I forget just how many blocks I had to walk—I was always obliged to rest at least once on the way, and to put the carpet-bags down for a minute or two on the steps of the hotel before going up to my room."

"And only two hundred thousand dollars in them?" cried Fred.

"Are greenbacks as heavy as that?" exclaimed Eugene.

"They made my arms ache, I assure you," replied Archie, "and I was glad when they were safe in the strong box at Cairo. Now, judging by that, how much do you think a million in small bills would weigh?"

"O, I'll not make a guess," said Featherweight. "I don't want to show how ignorant I am."

"Do you suppose you could lift it?"

"Well—no; could I?"

"Hardly; and to prove it to you, I will tell you a little circumstance. You perhaps remember that during the war the steamer Ruth was burned, having on board about four and a half millions of dollars, intended for the payment of the troops stationed along the river. She was supposed to have been set on fire by some members of the rebel secret service; but when it got abroad that the money was all lost, people began to accuse the paymasters who had charge of it with being in some way mixed up with its disappearance. Everybody knows that when a Mississippi river steamer gets on fire she burns like so much paper; but still there were those who thought that the money might have been brought off. Why didn't the paymasters—there were four of them, and that would have been just about a million apiece—save it while they were saving themselves? There were plenty of soldiers to guard it, and why didn't some of them catch it up and swim ashore with it? It could have been easily done, so people said, and the fact that it was not done started the story that the money was not on board the Ruth at all—the paymasters had pocketed it, and burned the boat to cover its loss.

"About this time it so happened that our chief went to St. Louis alone after money; but having forgotten the draft, he telegraphed to me to bring it up to him. I left Cairo on Sunday afternoon, and not being able to make connections at Odin, was obliged to stop over until the next morning. The only hotel in the town being full, the proprietor put me into a room with a gentleman in citizen's clothes, who had in his possession a cigar box which he handled as carefully as if it had been a torpedo. Having so valuable a piece of paper about me, I was, of course, somewhat particular as to the company I kept. I was naturally anxious to know something about my room-mate, and a reference to the hotel register showed me that he was an army paymaster. Of course, I felt perfectly safe in his presence after I found that out. I scraped an acquaintance with him, and he turned out to be one of the paymasters who was on board the Ruth when she was burned. Before we retired he showed me the contents of his box. It was the charred remains of a package of greenbacks which he had recovered from the wreck, and which he was taking to Washington to prove to the authorities there that the money had really been destroyed."

"Did he tell you why it was not saved?" asked Eugene.

"He did, and the reason was this: The money was packed away in four iron-bound boxes, each of which was so large and heavy that it took eight men to carry it from the forecastle up the stairs to the boiler deck where the money was kept under guard. Wouldn't a paymaster have looked nice swimming ashore with one of those boxes under his arm?"

The two boys gazed at Archie a moment in mute surprise, and then faced about with a common impulse and looked at the wagon behind them in which the emigrant said his treasure was stowed away. Whatever it was, it must have been something that did not weigh much, for the mules walked along easily and rapidly, and their traces were slack more than half of the time. The boys had learned something. Their curiosity had been aroused too, and they were impatient for the camping hour to arrive in order that they might, if possible, obtain a glimpse of the box containing the emigrant's wealth.   What could it be?   And with this inquiry arose another.   Since the emigrant had been so very imprudent as to tell Zack and Silas that he had something with him worth a million dollars, was not the vicinity of that wagon-train a dangerous place for them?   The boys began to think so, and to wish most heartily that they had never seen it.

CHAPTER III.

ARCHIE MAKES A TRADE.

THE last time we saw the Sportsman's Club, as we have already said—when we speak of the Club now we include all our friends who left Bellville in the *Stranger* for a voyage around the world —they were located in their camp a short distance from Fort Bolton, having just been joined by Dick Lewis and old Bob Kelly, the famous trappers, who held so high a place in the estimation and affections of Frank and his cousin Archie. All our friends now, from the old sailor down, had a warm place in their hearts for them, for it was by their assistance that Walter had been rescued from the most dangerous situation in which he had ever been placed.

It was not likely that the Club would ever forget the thrilling adventures through which they had so recently passed. If they desired to bring them more vividly to mind, all they had to do was to go up to the Fort and take a look at the outlaws, who were there confined in irons and under guard, or ride down the gully to Potter's rancho, where the final scenes in the drama had been enacted.

The Club never grew tired of visiting the rancho. They spent many an hour there, exploring every nook and corner of the building, and more than one article of plunder which had there been secreted, did they find and give into Colonel Gaylord's possession. Everything that had fallen to the share of Dick Lewis and old Bob had been carefully preserved, and was also given into the charge of the commandant, to be returned to its lawful owners, if they should ever be found. Each boy retained a few things of no particular value, to remind him of the robber band, and Frank kept the horse Potter had presented to him. He told the colonel how he came by him, and the colonel said it was all right. Frank had borne a prominent part in the exciting scenes that had transpired during the last few days, and the colonel probably thought it no more than right that he should be allowed to keep the horse, as a small reward for his services.

This horse was the occasion of a spirited controversy and rivalry, which straightway arose between the cousins, and was similar to that which had taken place when they first came upon the prairie, years ago. Frank thought much of his new acquisition, which was really a magnificent animal, and boasted of his qualities, while Archie made light of them, challenged him to a race, and was badly beaten for his pains. Then Archie borrowed every fast horse about the Fort that he could hear of, and ran him against the black, which left them behind, one and all, so easily that it was really provoking. Even Dick's fine nag, the one Frank had stolen out from under the rifles of the herders, and which his owner declared could not be beaten by anything that stood on four feet, was distanced, and Archie, Eugene and Featherweight—of course these two sided with Archie in everything—laid their heads together and declared that something must be done.

What that something was that ought to be done they could not make up their minds, until one day Eugene, who was strolling about the Fort, examining everything there with as much interest as though he had never seen it before, accidentally overheard a conversation between Frank and Lieutenant Gaylord which suggested something to him. There had been a race that morning between the cousins, Archie being mounted on Dick's horse, in which Frank as usual came out ahead, and he and the lieutenant, who were fast friends, were having a hearty laugh over it.

"That's a fine animal of yours, Nelson," said the young officer, "but there never was a horse yet so swift that some other couldn't beat him. I know where there are two, and I can put my hand on one of them almost any day, which can take him down in a mile race, as easily as falling off a log."

"Where are they?" asked Frank.

"One of them belongs to a one-eyed Indian who comes to the Fort occasionally. He is a mouse-colored animal, spotted all over with white, and

looks odd enough at a distance; but he is pretty
when you get close to him, and is as fleet as an
antelope."

"And the other?"

"He belongs to father; but he doesn't do him
much good, seeing that he has not set eyes on him
for three months."

"Was he stolen?" asked Frank.

"No; he escaped and joined a drove of wild
horses."

"Then there is no danger that Archie will get
hold of him."

"None whatever."

"And how about this Indian's horse? Couldn't
he buy him?"

"No. There isn't an officer about the fort who
has not tried to purchase him, but the owner will
not sell him. These Indians know a good horse
when they see him as well as a white man does.
They are like the Arabs. They will sell any of
their old hacks, but their best stock they keep for
their own use."

This was all Eugene could catch of the conversation, but it was quite enough to set him to thinking. He hurried back to the camp, to find Fred and Archie, and taking them off on one side, told them what he had heard.

"I only hope that horse will come about while we are here," said Archie.

"So do I," replied Eugene.   "We'll try our best to buy him.   It is no sign that we should fail because others have done so.   We may have something the Indian wants."

"Look there!" said Bob, suddenly calling to the three friends.   "Isn't that a queer colored blanket that man has spread over his horse?"

The boys looked and saw a horseman riding toward the fort.   A closer examination revealed the fact that he was an Indian; and a still closer inspection of the animal he rode satisfied them that what Bob had supposed to be a blanket, was not a blanket after all.   It looked more like a leopard skin.   Bob was the first to discover his error, or at least to speak of it.

"I declare," said he, as the Indian drew nearer, "I believe the spots are in the horse!"

"I know they are," whispered Eugene, excitedly. "Now if the man on his back is a one-eyed Indian, he's the very fellow we're looking for. Let's go and see."

The boys walked rapidly toward the Fort, but before they reached it the Indian had dismounted at the gate, where he was joined by Frank and Lieutenant Gaylord. The former seemed to be very much interested in the horse. He gave him a good looking over, passed his hands over his sleek skin, felt his legs, examined his mouth, and then put his hands into his pockets and stood off again and looked at him. His actions were enough to satisfy Archie and his two friends that they had not been mistaken in the horse. They slackened their pace and loitered along, to give Frank and the lieutenant time to finish their examination and get out of the way, and when they saw them go into the Fort they ran up and accosted the Indian. He had one eye and consequently, as Eugene declared, must be the man they wanted to see.

"Hallo, uncle," said Featherweight. "That's an odd-looking beast you've got there."

"Me chief, no uncle," said the Indian.

"Ah! all right. You Indians put one in mind of Artemas Ward's military company, you're all officers. I've never seen one of you yet who did not claim to be a chief. Where did you get him?"

"Injun raise him," replied the owner of the horse.

"He isn't good for much, is he? He looks as though he were made up of three or four horses of different colors."

"He good as three, four, half dozen," said the Indian. "Keep good."

"You don't care about selling him, do you?"

"Well, s'pose Injun sell, what you give?"

"O, I don't want him," said Fred. "I've got one that just suits me.

"I have a horse I'll trade for him," said Archie.

"How much boot will you give me? I know he is good, for I rode him all the way from Salt Lake City."

"Where he?" asked the Indian, looking around.

"O, he's down at the camp."

"S'pose you let Injun see him."

"All right, I will."

Archie walked off, whistling as he went, and acting altogether very unconcerned; but he was in reality highly excited. The Indian talked as if he might possibly be induced to trade, and the prospect of owning a horse that could beat his cousin's, was enough to put Archie in the best of spirits. He caught his nag, which was feeding near the camp, saddled and bridled him, and rode back to the Fort. He found his friends waiting for him on the other side of the stockade, where they had taken the Indian and his horse, so that Frank, if he should happen to come out, should not see what was going on. They intended to make the trade, if they could, and surprise him.

"There's a horse for you, chief," said Featherweight, as Archie rode up and dismounted. "If he isn't a good one I never saw one."

A grunt was the only reply the Indian made. Whether it was intended to express contempt, or something else, the boys did not know. He gave Archie's horse a good looking over, while the owner and his companions stood near, calm and indifferent to all outward appearance, but really very anxious, and impatient to hear his decision.

"Well, speak up," said Eugene, as the Indian, having completed his examination, stepped back to take a general survey of the horse. "Will you trade?"

"You got blanket?" asked the savage.

"O, we're not going to give you more boot than you can carry away—you may depend on that," said Featherweight.

"I wouldn't mind throwing in a pair of blankets," said Archie.

"Good?" asked the Indian.

"Yes, they'll be good. Not a hole in them."

"And to make you feel a little better over it,

perhaps we'll add a pipe or two and some tobacco,"
said Eugene.

" Five pounds ?"

" Yes ; we'll say five pounds."

" You got six-shooter short-gun ?"

No, Archie was quite sure he had no revolver
that he could spare. He had but two, and he
might need them before he saw home again. But
Eugene suggested that he might purchase a second-
hand weapon of the sutler, and after some debate
the point was conceded.

The bargaining thus commenced continued for
nearly half an hour, the Indian showing himself as
smart as any Yankee in a trade, sticking to his
points with so much pertinacity that the boys were
obliged to yield to every one of them, and finally
Archie left his companions in high glee and walked
into the Fort. When he came out again, a few
minutes afterward, he carried a pair of blankets
over his arm, an army revolver in his hand, and
his pockets were filled with tobacco, powder, lead,
cartridges, pipes and knives. The Indian critically

examined every article as it was passed over to him, and then after shifting his saddle to the back of Archie's horse mounted and rode off, leaving Archie holding fast to his new purchase and looking first at one and then at the other of his companions, who were so highly elated that they could scarcely restrain their glee until the Indian was out of hearing.

"We did it," said Featherweight, who was the first to speak.

"And so easily, too," added Eugene. "You got him cheap, Eugene, if he is as good as the lieutenant says he is. Your old horse cost you seventy-five dollars in Salt Lake, and the articles you bought of the sutler, being all second-hand, could not have cost you much more than twenty dollars. Ninety-five dollars is little money for a good horse."

Archie drew a long breath and looked at his nag with an expression of great satisfaction on his face, which, however, quickly changed to a look of anxiety as a disagreeable thought intruded itself upon him.

"Fellows," said he, "perhaps this isn't the horse we want at all. I have my suspicions. That Indian parted with him almost too willingly."

"Eh?" exclaimed Eugene. "O no, that can't be. The lieutenant said the horse was mouse-colored and covered all over with white spots, and that his owner was a one-eyed Indian."

"But if there should happen to be two mouse-colored horses about the Fort and two one-eyed Indians," said Fred, dolefully, "why then——"

"And another thing," continued Eugene, when Featherweight paused, "didn't we see Frank and the lieutenant looking at this very horse while we were on our way from the camp? That meant something, according to my way of thinking."

"If I have been cheated," said Archie, "I shall never hear the last of it."

"But you haven't been cheated," said Eugene. "Lend me the horse for about five minutes, and

you and Fred stay here till I come back.   I'll soon
settle the matter."

Archie's saddle and bridle were quickly put upon
the mustang, and then Eugene mounted him and
rode around an angle of the stockade into the
gate.

CHAPTER IV.

THE NEW HORSE.

AS Eugene rode through the gate the sound of laughter, which he knew came from the lieutenant's quarters fell upon his ear. Inside the apartment was gathered a gay party, consisting of the lieutenant, Frank Nelson and some of the younger officers of the Fort. The doors and windows were open, and they could see every thing that went on outside. The lieutenant was telling some amusing story, in the midst of which he suddenly paused, and jumping to his feet hurried to the door. Eugene saw him, but pretended he did not, and reining in his horse, began looking all about the Fort as if he were in search of somebody. The lieutenant said something in a low tone to those in the room, and in a second the doors and windows were filled with heads. That was quite enough to satisfy Eugene, who turned about and would have gone out again had not the lieutenant called to him.

"Hallo, there!" he exclaimed.

"Ah! glad to see you," said Eugene, riding up in front of the young officer's quarters. "Hope you are enjoying your usual good health. You haven't seen anything of Uncle Dick about here during the last hour or two, have you?"

"Whose horse is that?" demanded the lieutenant, without replying to the question.

"This?" said Eugene, innocently. "O, he's one Archie Winters picked up a short time ago. Do you know anything about him?"

"Archie hasn't bought him?" exclaimed the lieutenant.

"Well—yes; I believe so."

"Why, it can't be possible! What sort of a looking man was it he bought him of, do you know?"

"A one-eyed Indian," exclaimed Eugene, glancing through the door at Frank, whose face wore so comical a look of blank amazement that Eugene wanted to laugh outright. "Got him cheap, too—about ninety-five dollars."

"It is very strange, and I can't understand it," said the young officer, whose surprise seemed to increase every moment. "To my certain knowledge, that Indian has been offered three hundred dollars for this horse, time and again."

He came out to examine the animal, in order to make sure that he was not mistaken in him, and then went in again and held a whispered consultation with Frank; while Eugene once more made inquiries concerning his Uncle Dick, who, he knew perfectly well, was in camp enjoying his after-dinner smoke and nap. As he was about to ride away the lieutenant called to him again.

"I wish you would tell Archie that if he would like to dispose of that horse I'll give him a good trade," said he.

"I'll tell him, but I don't think he wants to sell. He needs a horse, and this one will perhaps suit him as well as any other."

"I should like to have him for a curiosity," added the lieutenant.

"That's what Archie wants him for, I believe—or something else. If you can't tell me where to find Uncle Dick, I guess I'll go.   Good-by."

Eugene rode away from the lieutenant's quarters demurely enough, but as soon as he was safe through the gate and out of hearing of Frank and the rest, he threw himself forward on the horn of his saddle and laughed so heartily that Fred and Archie, who were waiting for him behind an angle of the stockade, looked at him in amazement as he came up. Their faces brightened at once, for they knew he had good news to communicate.

"It is all right," said Eugene, as soon as he could speak. "If you want to see a crest-fallen set of fellows, just go and call on the lieutenant. He says he'll buy this horse if you want to sell him. He'd like to keep him for a curiosity."

"O, he would, would he?" said Archie. "I know a story worth two of that. I don't want to sell."

"Of course you don't. Now let's go down to camp, and after Fred and I have saddled our horses, we'll go out and have a gallop. I want to see this fellow move."

The others readily agreed to this proposition. The numerous defeats they had sustained in their efforts to make Frank "take a back seat," as they expressed it, had made them timid, and they wanted to know just what their new horse could do before they began boasting of his speed. The camp reached and the horses saddled, the three boys rode off and finally disappeared behind the swells.

The races that began as soon as they were out of sight of the camp and Fort continued for half an hour or more, each boy in turn riding the new horse; and the rapidity with which he moved over the ground when put to the top of his speed, and the ease with which he left the others behind, were enough to make the three friends dance with delight. They did not know that there were three persons who were watching their movements with a great deal of interest, but such was the fact. One of them was an Indian, who had thrown himself flat upon the summit of a neighboring swell, so that nothing but the top of his head could be seen above the grass, and the others were two horsemen who sat in their saddles in plain view of the racers. They were Frank and the lieutenant.

It was a great mystery to these two friends, not only how Archie had managed to possess himself of a horse which nearly every officer stationed at the Fort had tried in vain to purchase, but also how he had happened to hear of him. It was their intention to keep his existence a profound secret. It was a question in their minds, too, whether or not Archie knew what a prize he had secured; and in order to settle their doubts on this point, they mounted their horses and rode out to watch his movements.

"I am satisfied now," said the lieutenant, when he and Frank had witnessed two of the three races that came off. "If Archie didn't know that the horse was fast when he bought him, he certainly knows it by this time. It is all up with you, my boy."

"I shouldn't mind being beaten," said Frank, "only I have crowed over Archie a good deal, and he will pay me back a thousand fold. No one can beat him at that."

"There's no way to avoid it, that I can see, unless you catch that wild horse of father's. That would be a feather in your cap and money in your pocket. The race will take place to-morrow, I suppose."

"I suppose so," replied Frank.

But, as it happened, the race did not come off the next day, nor in fact on any day. An unlooked-for incident which happened that night saved Frank from defeat.

"Well, Archie," said Eugene, at the conclusion of the third race, during which the new steed, which was plainly growing tired of the sport, took the bits in his teeth and made a persevering attempt to run away with Featherweight, who was riding him, "if you never had a good horse before you've got one now, and Mr. Nelson will have to take a back seat, sure."

"But we don't want to run him against the black to-day," said Fred. "He's getting tired. We don't want to go back to camp either, for there's nothing interesting going on there; so how shall we pass the afternoon?"

"I don't know any better way than to follow up those antelopes again, if we can find them," said Eugene. "Perhaps we may succeed in bagging one of them."

This was the way the boys had passed a good portion of the week that had elapsed since the occurrence of the events at Potter's rancho. Archie knew something about antelope, and the manner of hunting them practised by the hunters of the prairies, and he had been initiating his friends into the mysteries of the sport. We mean by this that he had showed them how to attract the attention and excite the curiosity of the timid animals, by moving above the grass a red handkerchief attached to the muzzle of a rifle; but he had not yet shown them

4

how to shoot one, for the simple reason that the antelope, having been hunted and shot at by the officers and soldiers of the fort until their numbers had been pretty well thinned out, had become so wild and wary that Archie could never induce them to come within reach of his Maynard, which would have been sure death to one of them at six hundred yards. So in pursuit of the antelope the boys went; and the fact that during the whole of the afternoon they saw not the first sign of the game, did not dampen their ardor or detract from the pleasure of the brisk gallop they enjoyed. Neither would it in any way have marred their sport had they known that there was an eye watching all their movements; that it followed them in all their windings and turnings, and that when they rode into camp at c rk, the owner of it was not more than two hui lred yards behind them.

The Club's camp was permanently located upon the banks of a small stream which ran through a thickly-wooded dell about a quarter of a mile from the Fort. When they first pitched upon that spot

as a suitable camping-ground, they little thought
that that stream was one of the famous trout brooks
of which they had heard so much.   It had more
the appearance of the sluggish bayous so common
in Louisiana.   Its banks were low and marshy, the
water was muddy and almost too warm to drink,
the bed of the stream was filled with quicksands,
in which a horse and his rider would sink out of
sight, and taken altogether, one would as soon
expect to find alligators and water-moccasins there
as the speckled beauties in which anglers take so
much delight.   But the Club having explored the
stream almost to its source, knew that its fountain-
head was located among the hills about two days'
journey from the Fort; that for twenty miles the
brook was one succession of foaming cascades; and
that under every shelving rock along the banks was
a deep and silent pool in which the trout fairly
swarmed.   The strings of fish they caught there
were far ahead of anything Frank and Archie had
ever drawn from the brooks about Lawrence, and
two days' splendid sport made no apparent diminu-

tion in their numbers. There seemed to be just as many left, and they were so eager to be taken that they would snap at a naked hook.

But the Club could not spend all their time in fishing, however much they enjoyed the sport. They expected to remain at the Fort not more than two weeks longer (Dick had warned them that the mountain passes would soon be blocked with snow, and that if they intended to return to California before the winter set in, they had but little time to spare), and there was still much to be seen. They scoured the prairie and foot-hills for miles on each side of the Fort; knocked over sage hens and jack rabbits by the dozen; chased a young grizzly bear that had strayed down from the mountains, and obtained one or two shots at elk and black-tails; but there were two species of animals that were occasionally seen about the Fort which they had not yet been able to find—buffalo and wild horses. The buffalo had been driven off the range by the hunters, who, in order to procure their hides, slaughtered them at all seasons of the year, and wild mustangs, Dick said, were not as often met with as in the years gone by. He had not seen any for a long time. True there was a small drove of horses which was now and then seen in the neighborhood of the Fort, but the animals comprising it were not mustangs. They were from the States, and it was supposed that they had either strayed away from some emigrant train, or been stampeded by the Indians. Among them was a small bay horse, with black points and a white star in his forehead, which had once belonged to Colonel Gaylord. He had escaped from the herders, joined this half-wild drove, and having gained his liberty seemed determined to keep it. He was a valuable animal, and it was understood that his owner was ready to pay a handsome reward to any one who would capture and return him.

It had by this time become pretty well known that Archie had traded for a new horse during the day, and the Club were talking about it when he rode into the camp. As he dismounted in front of the fire there was a general setting down of plates, and a simultaneous rush made by all the boys, who were as eager to examine the new horse as his owner was to exhibit him. They knew that the animal had been purchased on purpose to beat Frank's horse, and they had a multitude of questions to ask about him.

"I suppose you two don't care to see him, do you?"

This question was addressed by Eugene to Frank and Dick, who kept their seats by the fire, and devoted their whole attention to their suppers.

"I have seen him once before to-day," said Frank.

"And what opinion have you formed regarding him?"

"I think he's a very good-looking old hack."

"O, do you?" exclaimed Archie. "It is very kind of you to say so much. But if you will take a ride with me to-morrow morning after breakfast, I'll warrant you'll think he is something besides an old hack before you see the last of him."

Every one present understood that this was

equivalent to a challenge, and Frank promptly accepted it as such, being resolved to " die game."

" Now, Dick, let's hear what you've got to say," continued Eugene.

" I hope you didn't give much for him," was the trapper's answer.

" Not much—a horse and about twenty dollars worth of blankets and things."

" I'm sorry you gin that much."

" Why ?   Isn't he worth it ?"

" I reckon he is."

" Then why are you sorry ?"

" O 'cause."

" That's no reason at all," said Fred.   " You're sorry the black is going to get beaten, but we can't help it.   We don't want to take dust all the time, and what's more, we don't intend to do it."

Dick made no reply.   He only smiled and glanced at old Bob, who gave him a significant look in return.   Archie saw it, and knew that Dick had some other reason for wishing the trade had not been made.   What it was he could not imagine.

He thought of a score of things while he was un-saddling his horse and staking him out with the rest, but could decide upon nothing. When he returned to the fire a well-filled plate was placed before him, and in taking part in the conversation and listening to the trappers' anecdotes, he soon forgot all about his new horse and the race that was to come off on the morrow.

CHAPTER V.

THE INDIAN TRADES BACK.

THE Club were tired that night, as indeed they were every night, and sought their blankets at an early hour.   Uncle Dick had undisputed possession of the little Sibley tent that was pitched on one side of the fire; Frank, Perk, Walter, George and Bab bunked in the wagon; Archie and his two friends slept under a brush "lean-to" which they had erected for their own especial benefit; and the trappers passed the night wherever they happened to be sitting or lying when sleep overpowered them. On this particular night Dick and old Bob sat up and smoked after all the rest of the party had retired—indeed until they had all fallen asleep except Archie.

The latter thought as much of his new horse as he had thought of his first pair of skates, which he

found in his stocking on a certain Christmas morning when he was about eight years old. For a
week or two after those skates appeared he never
went to bed without placing them on a chair close
by, so that they would be the first things his eyes
rested on when he awoke in the morning. He
would have been glad to do the same by the horse,
but as he could not, he contented himself with
lying awake and thinking about him; and thus it
happened that he overheard some conversation that
was not intended for his ears, and which was the
means of bringing him a hard fall and a jumping
headache, which he had for an inseparable companion all the next day. The conversation referred
to took place between the trappers. The camp had
been quiet for an hour, and old Bob, supposing that
everybody was asleep, removed his pipe from his
mouth long enough to say :

"I'm sorry the leetle 'un gin them blankets and
things fur that speckled hoss, 'cause he's sartin to
be jest that much out of pocket !"

"I know it," replied Dick.

" I was kinder in hopes you'd tell him," continued Bob.

" I thought of it, but what good would it a done ? The Injun in course sold him the hoss intendin' to steal it agin, an' we'd best let him take it now, an' without makin' no fuss about it, an' without his hurtin' the boy."

" Wal, mebbe so," said Bob.

" You see," added Dick, " if he can't steal him one time he will another. If he can't take him to-night, mebbe he'll ketch the youngster alone on the prairy to-morrer or next day, an' knock him down an' make off with the hoss ; an' that would be sartin to raise a rumpus ; 'cause if that Injun's head an' the sights of my rifle should ever come in line arterwards, the we'pon would go off whether I said so or not, an' then thar'd be one Injun less."

" I know ;" said Bob, " an' mebbe its best as it is. Let the Injun have his ole hoss, if he wants him."

Archie listened in amazement to this conversation and caught every word of it. He knew now why Dick was sorry that he had purchased the horse.   He remembered that the trappers had told him a dozen stories illustrative of the propensity on the part of the noble red man to drive a hard bargain in a horse trade, and after disposing of a valuable animal for all he would bring, to steal him at the first opportunity.   He knew too why the Indian could not be prevailed upon to sell the horse to any of the officers of the Fort.   They were familiar with all the tricks to which he and his kind were addicted, and the horse, once in their possession, would be so closely guarded that he could never get a chance to steal him again.   But Archie was a stranger to the prairie and its customs, and a boy besides, and the savage did not think he would run any risk in trading with him.

"And he didn't run any risk in dealing with me, either," said Archie, after he had spent a few minutes in thinking the matter over.   "But he will run some risk if he tries to steal that horse from me, as sure as he is an Indian.   I gave him all the boot he asked—it was a fair, square and honest trade, and he must stand to it."

Archie threw aside his blankets, drew one of his revolvers from its holster and made his way quickly and cautiously toward the place where his horse was picketed.   He held his weapon in readiness to defend his property, should occasion demand it, but there was no one there to dispute possession of it with him—that is, there was no one in sight.   There was some one, however, crouching close by in the grass—some one who saw all he did, and who followed behind him at a safe distance as he led the horse away and made him fast to a sapling, which stood in the outskirts of the camp and close beside the wagon.   Having done this, Archie removed his blankets, saddle and weapons from the cabin, rearranged his bed under the wagon, and laid down almost within reach of his horse, and in such a position that he could see the smallest object that might attempt to approach him.

"Now, then," said he, "if that Indian thinks he is smart enough to steal this horse, I am ready to undeceive him. He would stand a much better chance of getting him if he would return those articles I gave him and tell me he wants to trade back. I'd rather give up the horse than be obliged to stand guard over him night and day. But I'll keep him long enough to have at least one race with Frank, no matter what happens."

So saying, Archie settled himself into a comfortable position and prepared to go to sleep, intending to wake in time to defeat the Indian's nefarious designs, if he had any. He knew that when savages intend to make a descent upon a wagon-train, they come just before daylight, for it is generally darkest then, the fires have burned low and the emigrants sleep the soundest. It was about this time that Archie wanted to wake up; and if he succeeded in doing so, he would stand guard over his property until the whole camp was astir.

The excitement occasioned by the conversation he had overheard between the trappers kept him awake for a long time, but sleep overpowered him at last, and then Archie knew nothing for many an hour. The camp fire, which Dick had mended once or twice during the night, had almost died away, the moon was out of sight behind the hills, and the thick darkness which the savage likes best was fast settling down over the woods and surrounding prairie, when Archie suddenly became conscious that there was something going on near him. A faint, rustling sound, as if some one was trying to pass carefully through the bushes, aroused him. Just then a burning ember from the log back of the fire fell off, blazed up as brightly as a candle for a moment, and then went out, making the camp and all surrounding objects look darker by contrast. But Archie, whose eyes were wide open, had seen something in that instant of time. He had seen an Indian crouching in a thicket close to the root of the sapling to which his horse was tied.

Giving a loud yell to arouse the camp, Archie jumped to his feet, and making a blind dive in the direction of his horse succeeded in fastening upon the lasso with which he was tied to the tree. But it happened that the lasso was no longer fast to the tree; it was in the hands of the Indian, who, as active as a cat, sprang upon the horse before the

boy could come within reach of him. Archie
quickly bracing his feet gave the lasso a tremen-
dous jerk, believing that if the savage held fast to
it, he could pull him to the ground again. No
doubt he would have accomplished his object had he
had any one but an Indian to contend with. The
latter, much too cunning to be caught in any such trap,
allowed the lasso to run freely through his hands,
and Archie went staggering back against the wagon
wheel. Before he could recover himself the Indian
dashed his heels into the sides of the horse, which
sprang away at the top of his speed, and Archie was
thrown with great violence to the ground; while the
rawhide rope, which was still fast to the horse's
neck, was drawn so rapidly through his hands that
they were burned almost to a blister. It was a'l
over in much less time than we have taken to tell
it. Before any of the others, who had been awakened by Archie's loud yell, could come to his
assistance, the Indian had obtained possession of
the horse and was out of sight in the darkness.
Then the members of the Club began to bestir them-

selves. Uncle Dick pulled aside the door of the tent and looked out; Eugene and Fred, who missed Archie as soon as their eyes were open, began groping blindly for their rifles, under the impression that the camp had been attacked by the Indians and their friend carried off by them; the boys in the wagon quickly made their appearance; while Dick and Bob sat up and stared at one another with an expression on their faces which said very plainly that they had been expecting something of the kind.

"'Like a snow-flake on the river, one moment seen, then lost forever,'" murmured Archie, gazing in the direction his horse had last been seen.

"What's the matter?" asked all the boys, in a breath.

"His speckled hoss is gone," said Dick.

"Yes, he's gone," repeated Archie, holding his hands under his arms, as if they were very cold instead of very warm, "and I am a few dollars out of pocket."

5

"Stolen !" cried the Club, beginning to comprehend the state of affairs.

They stood motionless and speechless for a few seconds, as people almost always do when they hear any astounding piece of intelligence, and then each boy looked at his neighbor to see what he thought about it. Eugene, who had been bustling about the camp, in search of a certain piece of his property which he could not find, was the first to speak.

"Well, that is not so bad as it might be," said he. "Can anybody tell me where to look for my bridle ? We expected to have a race any how, you know, and it might as well come off now as a few hours later. Let's follow him and make him give up the horse."

"How are we going to do it ?" asked Archie, dolefully.

"Why, are there not enough of us to take it away from him if he shows fight ?"

"Perhaps so," said Frank, "but there are not enough of us to catch him. He is safe by this time, and we'll never put eyes on that horse again."

The trappers said Frank was right; that an attempt to recover the lost steed would only be time and energy wasted; and this put a stop to the frantic search for saddles, bridles and weapons, in which some of the Club were engaged. The pursuit and capture of a cunning Indian thief would, the boys thought, be something to talk about in after days, and they were loth to allow so fine an opportunity for distinguishing themselves to pass unimproved. It was hard, too, to give up that fine horse, of which they had expected such great things; but the trappers' word was law, and the Club, with much grumbling, and many hearty wishes that they might have the pleasure of meeting that Indian at some future time, threw down their bridles and gathered about Archie to hear the story of his encounter with the thief. When they had questioned him to their satisfaction, and the palms of his hands had, at Uncle Dick's suggestion, been thickly coated with soap, they went back to their blankets and finally fell asleep again.

Archie's slumber was not very refreshing. He

could not banish thoughts of his lost horse, his head
and hands throbbed, and when he managed to catch
a few winks of sleep, he dreamed of wild mustangs
and fights with Indians without number. By daylight his hands ceased to trouble him; but his head
reminded him of the hard fall he had received, and
he did not feel much like leaving his blanket. It
required something, however, much out of the ordinary run of events to wholly depress Archie's buoy-
ant spirits; and when Dick reported to him that
his old horse had been found grazing with the
others, he told himself that he was in some slight
degree recompensed for the loss he had sustained.
While he was washing his hands and face at the
brook he was joined by Fred and Eugene.

"Say, Archie," whispered the former, looking
all around to make sure that none of the rest of
the Club were within hearing, "Dick says he saw
those wild horses this morning."

"Did he?" said Archie, not in the least interested in the matter, although under almost any

other circumstances Fred's enthusiasm would have affected him at once.

"Yes.   Can't you go out and catch one?   We should like to see the operation, and Dick says you are first rate with the lasso."

"The colonel's horse is among them, you know," said Eugene.   "If you should happen to catch him you would make something by it."

"But I couldn't do it," replied Archie.   "If it were possible for anybody to catch him he would have been returned to his owner long before this time."

"Well, we can go out and look at them, can't we?   We have never seen any wild horses, you know."

Yes, Archie thought they might take a look at them if they could find them; so a very light breakfast was hastily dispatched, and the three boys mounted their horses and rode off, telling their friends who remained in the camp that they were going out to catch the colonel's horse, and that they were not coming back without him.

Before they had gone a hundred yards from the camp, Archie began to wish he had not started at all. He could not help thinking of the fleet, handsome animal that had carried him the last time he was in saddle. His old horse—the one the Indian left when he stole the other—was a shaggy, rough-looking fellow, but he was one of the best the Club owned. He had been Archie's almost constant companion ever since he left Salt Lake City; had carried him safely during that long, rapid gallop from the foot of the mountains to Fort Bolton, which had been undertaken by the Club as soon as it was found that Walter was missing, and the fact that he had borne the fatigue of the journey better than any of the other horses, Frank's alone excepted, had raised him considerably in the estimation of his owner. But with all his good qualities he had some bad ones, and the most noticeable one, just now, was his rough, clumsy way of getting over the ground. Archie had scarcely thought of it before, but having backed the Indian's mustang, which was a remarkably easy riding horse, he thought of it now, and told himself that it was very disagreeable.

But one could not long remain in a gloomy frame of mind while he had the fresh, invigorating air of the prairie to breathe, and two such jolly fellows as Fred and Eugene for companions, and after he had been half an hour in the saddle Archie began to feel more like himself. Having as yet discovered no traces of the wild horses the boys began to give up all hopes of finding them, and allowing their animals to settle into a slow walk they rode side-ways, "woman fashion," to relieve their cramped limbs, and talked of the sports and adventures they had thus far seen since leaving Bellville, and speculated upon those yet to come. Finally, when the sun began to show himself above the hills, Fred broke out into a song, in which the others joined, and the result of which was rather surprising.

" ' The bright, rosy morning peeps over the hills,
   With blushes adorning the meadows and rills ;
   While the merry horn calls come, come away,
   O, wake from your slumbers and hail the new day.

" ' The stag roused before us away seems to fly,
   And pants to the chorus of hounds in full cry.
   Then follow the musical chase,
   Where pleasure and vigor and health all embrace.

   The day's sport, when over, makes blood circle right,
   And gives the brisk——' "

" Listen ! listen !" cried Archie, suddenly.

The boys brought their song to an abrupt ending, and drawing up their horses gazed at one another with faces full of wonder.

CHAPTER VI.

EUGENE'S PLAN.

THE three friends were at that moment approaching the summit of a high swell, and the noise which interrupted their song came from the other side. It was an indistinct, muffled sound, and so very much like that made by a heavily loaded wagon when rapidly driven, that they looked toward the top of the swell, more than half expecting to see a runaway team come quickly into view and dash down among them. But the noise grew fainter instead of increasing in volume, and after listening a moment the boys urged their horses forward and rode rapidly to the top of the swell. Then they found that the sound was occasioned by a drove of horses which had heard their voices, and were taking themselves off with all the speed of which they were capable. Featherweight uttered a cry of delight, but quickly followed it up with an ejaculation of disappointment.

"I was in hopes they were the wild horses," said he.

"And so they are," returned Archie.

"Why, they don't act as if they were very wild," said Eugene. "See how they shake their heads, and kick up their heels! Many a time have I seen our own horses playing that way in the pasture."

"No matter; they are the ones we are looking for; and that leading horse belongs to the colonel. I've heard him described often enough to know him."

At first Archie's companions could hardly believe it. Although the horses ran rapidly they did not act as if they were frightened, but pranced and curveted as if they were moved by the same spirit of mischief that sometimes possesses a domestic horse, when he flourishes his heels and retreats to the farthest corner of the pasture, as he sees his owner coming to catch him. But there was the colonel's horse! There was no denying his identity, for the boys all knew him as soon as they saw him. The wild steeds ran to the top of the nearest swell, faced about and looked at the horsemen, snorted once or twice, and then went to grazing as if nothing had happened.

"There they are," said Archie, "and now what are we going to do—take a good look at them and go back to camp?"

"No," replied Featherweight. "We'll give them a race of a mile or two, just to be able to tell our friends that we have chased a drove of wild horses. What do you say, Eugene?"

"Why," replied the latter, after a little hesitation, "I say that I have a plan in my head regarding those horses, if you will help me carry it out."

"Of course we will," said Archie. "Anything for fun. That's what we came out here for."

"It will keep us out on the prairie for three or four days and nights," continued Eugene.

"Then one of us had better go back to camp after our blankets," said Archie. "It is getting cold, and we'll freeze without some covering. Besides, if Dick is anything of a prophet, it will not be many days before we shall find the ground covered with snow. We shall need some food, too, and a supply of ammunition."

"You're sure you won't laugh at me if my plan fails," said Eugene.

"Certainly not."

"Well, then, I'll go back to camp after the things we need, if you and Fred will stay and keep an eye on the horses."

This plan being readily agreed to, Eugene turned and rode off at a gallop, while Fred and Archie dismounted and prepared to pass the time as pleasantly as they could until his return. They hobbled their horses with their lariats, to prevent them from running off to join the wild drove, turned them loose to graze, and seated themselves on the ground to watch the mustangs.

Eugene had partly developed what he considered to be a grand scheme for the capture of at least one of the wild horses. He had been thinking of it ever since he first heard of the existence of the drove, and he had finally hit upon something which seemed to hold out bright promises of success. He had read somewhere that wild horses had been captured by being kept in motion day and night, and allowed no opportunity to take food, water or rest. Of course the swiftest and strongest animal would soon wear out under such treatment, and when exhausted by long-continued exertion, and weak from protracted fasting, he could be easily run down and lassoed, and still he would be in nowise injured. A day or two of rest and good care would restore him to full health and vigor. Eugene had heard much of the speed of the colonel's horse and the fruitless attempts that had been made to capture him, and this plan of his seemed to be just the thing. He thought it over in all its details while he was on his way to the camp, and believed that he could see his way clearly. He provided for every contingency, and told himself that he knew just what to do in any emergency that might arise. But after all, he found, to his great surprise, that there was one very important matter that he had forgotten to take into consideration.

Eugene found the camp deserted by all save Dick and old Bob. These two were almost always to be found there. They had worked hard, had seen much excitement and met with many adventures during their sojourn at Potter's rancho, and were taking a good rest after it. They told Eugene that Uncle Dick was visiting with the colonel at the Fort, and that the rest of the Club had gone up the brook fishing.

"When they come back, whar'll I tell 'em you've gone?" added Dick, seeing that Eugene was busily engaged in gathering up various articles that were lying about the camp. "I want to know wharabouts to look for you when you're wanted."

"Well, you'll find us somewhere along the foot of the mountains between here and the Missouri river," replied Eugene. "That's not very definite, I admit, but I can't come any nearer answering your question. We have found those horses!"

"Wal?" said the trapper.

"And we're going to bring one of them back with us."

"Sho!" exclaimed Dick. "You haint agoin' to racin' with them critters, be you?"

"No, indeed. We know better than that. We are going to drive them down."

Dick looked at Bob as if wondering whether or not he had heard aright, and then arose and approached Eugene.

"What did you say you was goin' to do?" he asked.

"I don't know what you call it," answered Eugene, "but we're going to keep those horses in motion until they're tired out, and then we're going to catch one of them."

"Youngster," said the trapper, lowering his voice as if he were afraid that some one might overhear what he was about to say, "that's the only way the colonel's hoss can be ketched."

"Then we can do it, can't we?" exclaimed Eugene, delighted to hear his plan endorsed by so high an authority.

"Sartin. Me an' ole Bob's jest been talkin' about it. Now, how are you goin' to work it?"

"Why, we're going to take after them and follow them up until we tire them out, and then Archie will ride up and lasso one of them."

Dick looked down at the ground and meditated a moment.

"I don't reckon I see through it quite," said he. "You don't say nothing about restin' your own horses an' yourselves."

"Eh!" exclaimed Eugene.

"While you're tirin' out the wild hosses won't your own get tired out too, if you don't give 'em a chance to eat an' rest?"

Eugene's hopes fell instantly. This was the important part of his plan that he had not thought of. Of course if the wild steeds were to be "driven down," it was necessary that their pursuers should occasionally be mounted on fresh horses, or else the chances were that by the time the mustangs were exhausted, their own nags would be in no better condition.

" Did you say anything to the leetle 'un about this?" asked Dick presently.

" Who? Archie? No. I've kept it to myself."

" Then that 'counts fur it. I didn't think he'd go in fur sich a thing, 'cause he knows it can't be did; an' so will you arter you think it over. Howsomever, I'll tell you what you can do: You see—but if you go you'll have to camp out fur three or four nights—mebbe six or seven."

" We don't care for that. We'll be prepared, you see," said Eugene, pointing to the bundle he was making up.

" An' won't your uncle care, nuther?"

" No. He knows that we used to camp out in the swamps of Louisiana for weeks at a time."

" An' you won't be afraid when you hear the coyotes a yelpin' an' a howlin' around you of nights, and you all alone on the prairy?"

" Of course not. We've heard wolves before we ever saw the prairie."

" Wal, go ahead if you're so sot onto it. The leetle 'un can take keer of himself an' you too;

but if so be you should happen to get into any difficulty, as you'd be sartin to do if that keerless Frank was along, mebbe me an' ole Bob'll be around. An' as fur drivin' them hosses——"

Here the trapper proceeded to give Eugene some very explicit directions as to the manner in which he ought to proceed in order to make his experiment successful; but we will not stop to repeat them, as they will all appear as our story progresses.

Eugene listened attentively, and after satisfying himself that he fully understood his instructions, he gathered up his friends' blankets and his own, together with a goodly supply of bread and meat, some ammunition for Archie's Maynard and his Henry rifle and Fred's, a hatchet and a few other articles he thought they might need, and strapping them in a bundle behind his saddle, mounted his horse and rode gayly out of the camp. He laughed when he thought what a great mistake he had made in laying out his first plan, and felt more certain of success than ever. The trapper had assured him that failure was next to impossible if the matter were rightly managed, and Eugene began to enjoy in anticipation the reception that would be extended to him and his companions when they rode into camp with the captured horse. Of course they didn't want any reward for restoring him to his owner, and wouldn't accept any. If the colonel would allow them to keep him a day or two, just long enough to run a few races and take a little of the conceit out of Frank, they would be abundantly satisfied.

A few minutes' ride brought Eugene to the top of the swell where he had left his friends, but they were not there. The wild steeds had moved nearer to the hills during his absence, and Archie and Fred had followed in order to keep them in sight. Eugene set up a loud shout and presently heard a faint response. After repeating the call, to make sure of the direction in which his friends had gone, he rode down the swell and in a quarter of an hour joined his companions and found them in their saddles slowly following the mustangs, which were moving in a body toward the distant mountains.

The first thing Eugene did was to distribute the ammunition he had brought with him and to divide his bundle, which was rather too bulky for one horse to carry. While he was thus engaged his friends reminded him that he had not yet told them what his plan was; so Eugene went into details, to which the boys listened eagerly, and said in conclusion:

"Dick assures me that if we keep the horses moving, we ought to travel at least twenty-five miles between daylight and dark, and that will bring us to the mountains the day after to-morrow. We must keep them walking all the time, but we must not push them too closely, for if we frighten them they will run away from us and we may never see them again. If we keep them travelling as nearly north-west as we can, we shall discover, when we come within sight of the mountains, a tall, iso-lated rock, which, at a distance, looks exactly like a chimney. Close to the foot of this rock is a gully, which leads to a beautiful valley about twenty miles back in the mountains. Dick says that is the horses' stamping-ground, and if we can make them go in there we've got them sure. This valley is about ten miles in circumference, and has no outlet except the gully before spoken of; and all we've got to do is to make our camp right in the mouth of this gully, so that they can't get out, and then relieve one another in the work of driving the horses down."

"Then we shall not really begin business until we reach this valley?" said Featherweight.

"No," replied Eugene. While we are on the prairie the wild horses will have the same chance to eat and rest that ours will; but when we once get them cornered we'll fix them. What do you think of it, any how?"

The boys were loud in their praises of the scheme, and Archie, who had often read of such things, wondered he had not thought of it before.

During the next two days nothing transpired worthy of note. The boys steadily followed the wild steeds, which finally seemed to become somewhat accustomed to their presence. During the first few hours they were very restive, and on several occasions, when the boys in their eagerness followed them a little too closely, they took to their heels and left them far behind. They turned out of the way once or twice for water, but kept the same general course, and on the afternoon of the third day brought their pursuers within sight of the landmark the trapper had described to them.

CHAPTER VII.

THE WILD MAN OF THE WOODS.

DICK LEWIS had warned Eugene that constant vigilance was to be the price of his success, and among other things had told him that, before his expedition was ended, he might discover that horses were the most obstinate and contrary things in the world. The drove could probably be driven very easily, he said, until they reached the entrance to the gully; and then, if they found that they were expected to enter it, the chances were that they would take to their heels, leaving their pursuers nothing to do but to make the best of their way back to the Fort. Eugene, remembering the warning, took measures to prevent so abrupt an ending to their hunt. He sent Archie out on one flank and Fred on the other, with instructions to head off the horses, should they attempt to escape,

while he himself followed after them as before.
But it happened that no very serious difficulty was
experienced, and everything would have worked
smoothly but for an unlooked-for incident that
occurred, and which they could not have guarded
against, even had they been expecting it.

The horses had been without water all day, and
knowing probably that there was none to be found
nearer than the valley toward which they were
heading, they kept straight on at a rapid walk,
turning neither to the right nor left, and in an
hour more were fairly between the two high hills
which marked the entrance to the gully. These
hills were two or three miles apart. A few hundred
yards farther on the gully proper began, and was
not more than a quarter of a mile wide. Once in
there, they were safe. Then the work would begin
in earnest. The spring which watered the valley
was located at the other end of the gully, twenty
miles away in the mountains, and Eugene, who was
the acknowledged leader of the expedition, had told
his companions that the drove must not be allowed

to stop there to drink. The wild steeds had travelled at least twenty-five miles that day, with no nourishment except the few mouthfuls of grass they had been able to snatch as they passed along, and some of them acted as if they would like to stop and rest. If the boys camped that night as usual, the horses would doubtless pass on to the spring, refresh themselves with a good drink, eat their fill of the luxuriant grass growing about, take a good rest, and by the time their pursuers reached the valley, which would be on the afternoon of the following day, the wild nags would be ready for a long and hard test of endurance. In order to prevent this the council of war, which Eugene called, decided that no camp should be made that night. They would follow the drove through the gully, drive it on past the spring, and while two of their number made the camp and took rest and refreshment, the other would keep the horses in motion.

Archie thought their plans had been laid with considerable skill. He was on the right flank of the drove, which the boys called the post of honor, for there was some responsibility connected with it. If the horses became contrary and declined to enter the gully, the probabilities were that they would attempt to run by it instead of turning back, and in that event Archie was expected, if he could not head them, to capture one of the drove; for the boys were resolved that they would not go back to the Fort without catching something, and in order to make the agreement more binding, they had shaken hands on it.

Archie was prepared for anything that might happen. He had put himself in the lightest possible running order, by giving his bundle and weapons to his companions, and discarding his jacket and hat. He had tied a handkerchief over his head to keep his hair out of his eyes, and rode along with his lariat in his hand and his gaze fastened upon the leader of the drove. In his eagerness to approach as close to him as he could, he kept his horse in a fast walk, and in this way gradually drew ahead of some of the laggards of the drove, who, fearing that they were about to be cut off from their companions, broke into a gallop. This set the whole drove in motion. They went ahead at the top of their speed, holding straight for the gully, and Archie, believing that he should have no use for his lasso that day, was about to tie it fast to the horn of his saddle, when he saw the leading horses suddenly swerve from their course, and then stand motionless, gazing at some object before them that had attracted their attention.

Archie looked, and saw something crouching behind a tree on one side of the gully. He put his hand to his side where he usually carried his field-glasses, but he had given them with the rest of his accoutrements into the keeping of his friends. Then he shaded his eyes with his hand and looked again, and after a few seconds' close inspection made out that the object was a human being, and not a wild animal, as he had at first supposed. And a most forlorn looking specimen it was too, unless his eyes greatly deceived him. It wore the most dilapidated suit of clothes that Archie had ever seen; its feet looked like two small barrels, being wrapped in blankets or hides, no doubt, and from under something on its head, which might once have been called a hat, the long unkempt hair was sticking in every direction. Archie did not get a good glimpse of its face, and indeed he did not think to try. His mind was fully occupied with the horses. Forgetting every thing except that the frightened animals were on the point of taking to their heels, and thereby causing him and his companions the loss of three days' hard work, Archie called to the man, for such he believed the apparition to be.

"Say, you!" he shouted. "Couldn't you step back out of sight a moment, long enough to allow these horses to pass you?"

The figure complied with a readiness that was surprising. As if frightened by the sound of his voice, it disappeared on the instant, and made a most precipitate retreat up the hillside, if one might judge by the shower of stones that came rattling down among the bushes. The noise frightened the horses worse than ever. The leaders turned back upon those behind them, and for a few seconds they were mixed up in great confusion, some pressing one way and some the other. Archie believing that the hunt was virtually over, and that he and his friends were to have nothing but their trouble for their pains, determined to make one bold stroke to save their fortunes. In response to a touch from the spurs his horse sprang forward, the wild steeds parting right and left before him, and with a few rapid bounds carried his rider into the very midst of the drove.

Fred and Eugene had stopped at the first sign of commotion among the wild horses, not knowing how to account for it and utterly at a loss what to do. Being willing to leave the management of affairs entirely in Archie's hands, they sat in their saddles and watched his motions with the greatest interest. When they saw him dashing into the drove, and his lasso flying from his hand, uncoiling itself as it went, their joy knew no bounds.

"The hunt is over," shouted Eugene, in great glee. "Dick says he doesn't miss his aim once in a hundred times."

"Then this throw must be the unlucky one," said Fred, in reply, "for he has certainly missed."

When Fred spoke Archie's horse was standing motionless, and his rider was hauling in his lasso hand over hand. If he had failed in one thing he was successful in another, for his sudden charge had assisted the horses to decide a point they were unable to decide for themselves. It showed them that the only safe way of retreat was toward the gully, and into it they went with all the speed of which they were capable, every one of them giving a wide berth to the tree behind which had stood the object that occasioned their alarm. Fred and Eugene, although greatly disappointed, had seen a sight they would not have missed for a good deal. They had seen a lasso thrown at a wild horse, and that was something to put into the next letter they wrote to their friend Wilson. When they came up with Archie they found him bent half double, holding his horse by the bridle and peeping up under the bushes which covered the side of the gully.

" Well, you didn't catch him, did you ?" exclaimed Eugene.

" No, but I did my best, and if my lariat had been a little longer, I'd have had a different story to tell, for I made as straight a throw for his head as I ever made in my life. But I am encouraged after all. I know that my horse has had good training and can be depended on. When the lasso left my hand he stopped as if he had been shot. If I can only get another chance like that the bay is ours."

" Has one of them gone up there ?" asked Fred, seeing that Archie was still peering under the bushes.

" What was it that made such a commotion among them ?" inquired Eugene.

" The horses have all gone on down the gully, but the thing that frightened them went up here," replied Archie.

" What was it ?"

" The Wild Man of the Woods."

" The what ?"

"Well, I wish you had seen him—for I don't know what else to call him. He stood here behind this tree, and the sight of him turned the horses and frightened them so badly that I was afraid they were going to run away from us."

"Was it a man?"

"I judge so. He certainly was not an animal, for he was dressed; but he acted like an animal, for when I spoke to him and asked him to get back out of sight, he went up the hill on all-fours like a streak."

"There's something been up there, sure enough," said Eugene. "The fresh dirt on those stones shows that they have but recently been dislodged from their bed."

"What could it have been?" asked Fred, greatly astonished.

"Ask me something hard," replied Archie. "If there had been a menagerie along here lately, I should say that one of the gorillas had stolen a suit of the keeper's clothes and decamped. I have heard of wild men, but I never saw one before, and I have no desire to make his acquaintance. Whoever he is. he had better visit some trader pretty soon, or go to hunting furs, for his clothes will not last him much longer."

"Well, what's to be done about it ?"

"Nothing," answered Eugene. "We're hunting wild horses, and I suggest that we leave the wild men to take care of themselves."

"That's my idea," said Archie, springing into his saddle; "so let's jog along and keep the drove moving. The sun says it is pretty nearly supper time; so I think I'll take a bite. But, fellows, I should really like to know what that thing was."

The others said they would like to know too. There was much speculation indulged in, and Archie was required to describe the object and its actions again and again; and after each description his companions shook their heads, as if to say that the matter was too deep for them, and applied themselves with renewed energy to the bread and meat and flasks of cold tea which they drew from the pockets of their shooting-jackets. They could not explain it after half an hour's debate, and they finally came to the conclusion that they did not know anything about it and never would. After that nothing was said on the subject, although they did not cease to think about it, and each boy smiled at his neighbor when he saw him looking toward the top of the cliffs which hung over the gully, for he knew that he was looking to see if there were any signs of the wild man.

By the time their supper was over (they had eaten it as they rode along), they again came up with the wild horses, which, having recovered from their fright, were moving steadily on down the gully, stopping only to take occasional bites at the grass which grew in little bunches at the foot of the cliffs. It was almost dark now, and the boys, as they twisted about in their hard saddles, trying to find a comfortable position for their aching limbs, thought of the twenty long miles yet before them, and wished for a roaring fire and a soft, warm blanket. And these twenty miles were to be ridden during the night, through a gorge with which they were entirely unacquainted.   There might be a thousand perils and obstacles in their way.   Some savage beast, like Old Davy, might have an ambush in there somewhere, or their path might lead along the edge of some deep long chasm, where a single slip on the part of their horses would send them to destruction.   Archie was somewhat hardened to such things, but his companions were not, and when it is known that Eugene was the one who planned and suggested this night ride, it will be seen that he was resolved to accomplish something.

In less than twenty minutes after the sun went down a deep gloom began to settle over the gorge, and in twenty minutes more it was so dark in there that the boys could not discern the nearest objects. The wild horses were close before them, following a well-beaten path in Indian file, but the boys could not see them.   They were obliged to trust entirely to the animals they rode, and these, in turn, trusted to the leader of the drove.   The boys beguiled the weary hours with song and story, awaking a thousand echoes in the gorge and no doubt startling more

than one wild beast which was going his nightly
rounds. But, what was very surprising, the wild
horses, after the first few minutes, seemed to pay
no attention to their voices. Only once were they
frightened, and that was when a violent rustling in
a thicket of bushes at the foot of the cliff, drew a
couple of shots from Eugene's rifle. Then they
galloped on in advance, but were again overtaken
at the end of half an hour, and their pursuers kept
close company with them until daylight—so close,
in fact, that Eugene's nag received one or two
admonitory kicks from the last horse in the line.

The night passed at length, to the boys' great
relief, and the morning sun began to gild the sum-
mits of the surrounding mountains. His rays
gradually found their way into the gorge which just
here was as straight as if it had been cut out for a
railroad, and about a mile in advance of them the
boys saw the valley into which it opened. The
horses saw it too, and gradually quickened their
pace to a rapid walk, then to a trot, and finally to a
gallop; but their pursuers kept close behind, Archie

leading the way. Their object now was to drive them beyond the spring, which Dick told them they would find at the end of the gorge; and Archie, thinking that he might possibly have another opportunity to try his lasso on the bay, handed his bundle and weapons to his friends, and pressed close upon the rear of the drove. Furthermore, he anticipated the very thing that happened—a momentary confusion about the spring, which Eugene, from the information the trapper had given him, was able to describe so accurately that Archie knew just where to look to find it, and a chance to use his lasso, which, if quickly improved, would save them a day or two of hard work. Archie noticed that the horses were not nearly as wild as they had appeared to be when they first found them. They had grown more and more accustomed to the presence of their pursuers as the days went by, and now, having passed the night in their immediate company, they seemed to pay no more attention to them than they did to the members of the drove. Archie could not decide whether this indifference was the result of fatigue or increasing confidence; but whatever it was, he was ready to take advantage of it. In order to see just how far he could go, he turned his horse out on one side, and to his great gratification and the no small surprise of his companions, galloped along side by side with the rear horses in the drove, which, if they felt any displeasure at this familiarity, showed it only by laying back their ears and biting at his horse.

Archie gradually urged his nag forward, and before the valley was reached he had passed more than half the drove, and was riding within fifty yards of the bay which looked over his shoulder at him occasionally, but did not increase his speed or show any alarm. He was heading straight for the spring. Archie began to tremble with excitement. One after the other the members of the drove were passed, and at length only three horses were running between Archie and the leader. Just then the bay turned quickly out of the path, and in a moment more was standing knee-deep in the spring which bubbled out from under the cliff.

ARCHIE CAPTURES THE WILD HORSE.

And now happened the event for which Archie was looking and for which he was prepared. The other horses crowded in upon the bay—his own would have followed had he not restrained him—and in less time than it takes to tell it the spring was full of rearing, kicking, biting animals. But they were not permitted to remain there long. The leader began to assert his authority. Raising his head with an angry snort, he sent his heels right and left to such good purpose that he quickly cleared a space about him. The instant that his head was elevated was enough for Archie. The lariat left his hand, true to its aim this time, and settling down over the bay's neck was quickly drawn tight. Finding himself fast, the horse started to run, but the other end of the lasso was securely fastened to Archie's saddle, and his own horse bracing himself to meet the shock, the captured steed was thrown flat on his side. The others snorted with terror and took to their heels in short order.

When Fred and Eugene arrived upon the ground they saw something exciting.

CHAPTER VIII.

THE EMIGRANT TRAIN.

"HURRAH for you, Archie!" shouted Eugene, as he and Fred came galloping up. "You've made sure work this time, haven't you?"

"I told you that if I got another fair chance at him he was mine," replied Archie. "You had a suspicion that I was shooting with a long bow, last night, when I told you that I had seen a horse help his master catch cattle, didn't you, Fred?"

"No," returned Featherweight, quickly. "I only thought it something wonderful."

"I told you I had seen a horse hold a steer down while his owner butchered him, didn't I?"

"Yes," answered Fred.

"Well, now you will see my horse hold this fellow down while I put a bit in his mouth. Look out, there," he added, as the boys, having dismounted, ran up to watch his movements; "don't come too near his heels, for he can out-kick a mule. Keep a good hold of your own horses too, or they'll go off to join the drove."

Archie's nag, as his owner afterward declared, had shown himself to be a "perfect trump." He seemed to know what the boy intended to do as well as the boy knew it himself. When the lariat settled down over the bay's head and the latter was about to run off, he planted his fore-feet firmly on the ground to stop him, and the bay was thrown on his side, as we have described. Archie's horse, without waiting for the word from his rider, quickly backed up until the lariat was drawn tight, and thus the bay was held as securely as if he had been tied to the ground.

Archie, finding that his horse could be depended on, quickly dismounted, slipped the bridle off his head, and when Fred and Eugene came up he was kneeling on the bay's neck, trying to force the bits into his mouth.

"You're not going to ride him now, are you?"

exclaimed Fred, amazed at Archie's apparent reck-
lessness.

"Certainly I am," was the reply. "He's got to
be backed some time, and it might as well be now as
to-morrow."

"How are you going to get a saddle on him?
You can't put the girth around him while he is
lying down."

"I don't want any saddle!"

"Why, he'll throw you and break your neck!"

"If he does it shan't cost him anything,"
answered Archie, as he buckled the throat-latch
about the bay's neck. "Now, Fred, slack up on
that lariat, please, and give us room according to
our size and importance. We shall need plenty of
space to spread ourselves in!"

Fred, in compliance with the request, unfastened
the rawhide rope from Archie's saddle, and then he
and Eugene, still holding fast to their horses and
leading Archie's, retreated quickly to the foot of
the cliffs. As soon as Archie saw that they were
out of the way, he removed his weight from the

bay's neck, and in an instant the captured horse was on his feet. How Archie managed to get upon his back as he was rising was a great mystery to the two boys who were looking on — it was done so quickly. But he was there, and he had secured a firm seat, too.

The bay was no sooner on his feet than he began to make the most desperate attempts to shake off his rider, but all to no purpose. When he reared, Archie pounded him between the ears with his clenched hand; and when he kicked, he used his spurs with such hearty good-will that the horse was glad to desist. During all the terrific struggle Archie was as cool as a cucumber and was never once moved from his seat. Failing in his efforts to throw his rider, the bay tried to run, and this Archie not only permitted, but encouraged. There were two well-beaten paths at this point, one running to the right and the other to the left around the valley, and when the bay showed a desire to try his speed his rider turned him into one of these paths and touched him gently with the lariat, which he had managed to gather up, and now held in a coil in his right hand. The horse responded on the instant, and with a few rapid bounds carried Archie out of sight behind the trees. The boys stood listening to the sound of his hoofs for a moment, and then turned and looked at each other.

"That is something I never saw done before," said Eugene, at length.

"And if anybody had told me that it could be done, I wouldn't have believed him," added Fred. "He will probably go on around the valley, and as that is a good ten-mile ride, we shall have plenty of time to make the camp and get something to eat before he returns."

The boys watered the horses at the little brook that ran from the spring, staked out their own animals (having no lasso with which to picket Archie's horse they hobbled him with a halter so that he could not stray far away) and then went to work to prepare breakfast. From one of the bundles Fred brought to light a small sheet-iron camp-kettle, a coffee-pot and a hatchet. While he was undoing another, which contained the small supply of bacon and hard-tack they had remaining, Eugene picked up the hatchet, and in a few minutes had split up dry wood enough to start a roaring fire. The camp-kettle was filled with water from the spring, several slices of bacon placed around the fire on spits to roast, and then the two boys threw themselves on their blankets to take a few minutes' rest after their twenty-four hours in the saddle, and to await Archie's return.

He came much sooner than they expected, and they saw at a glance that that ten-mile gallop had taken considerable of the wild spirit out of the bay. He looked as if he had been driven through a stream of water; his breast was flecked with foam, and, although he still kept his ears laid back close to his head and showed a good deal of the white of his eye, he did not kick and plunge as he had done at starting, and seemed quite willing to stop when his rider gave him the word.

"Well?" said both the boys at once.

There was a good deal of meaning in that little

word, and Archie rightly interpreted it. Fred and Eugene were anxious to know if their new horse was swift enough to beat the black.

"I don't know," replied Archie, drawing his shirt-sleeve across his forehead; "I am not yet prepared to say. The horse was tired when he got here, and as the path around the valley is rocky and full of logs and brush, he didn't have a chance to show himself. But he moves as if he were set on springs and clears a good stretch of country at a jump, and there is no telling what he may do after he has had a good rest. Want to try him, either of you?"

"Well, n—no," replied Fred, with so comical an expression that Archie and Eugene laughed outright. "I believe I've ridden far enough for one day."

"Then I'll walk him up and down till he gets cooled off a little," said Archie. "After that we'll tie him to a tree and blanket him. In the meantime, if you don't know what else to do, you might cook some breakfast."

"We've cooked one breakfast and eaten it,"

said Eugene. "We were too hungry to wait for you."

"We'll have to send somebody out on a foraging expedition pretty soon," said Fred, holding up all that was left of the bacon. "To-morrow will see the last of our provisions, unless we put ourselves on short rations."

Fred set about his cooking operations again, while Eugene reclined on his blanket and watched Archie as he rode the bay slowly back and forth. Having once been thoroughly broken to saddle, the animal was still "bridle-wise," but, although he understood every command of his rider, he did not like to yield obedience. He preferred freedom to slavery and needed constant watching, for he was ready to take advantage of the smallest chance that was given him for escape. He was a very handsome, stylish animal, and it was no wonder that Colonel Gaylord did not like to give him up. When the bacon and coffee were ready, Archie hitched his horse in a thicket of evergreens, where he was effectually protected from the cold wind that was blowing, threw a blanket over him and went to breakfast.

The boys spent one day and night in their camp in the valley, during which the bay received the best of care and fully recovered from his fatigue, although he did not appear to become reconciled to captivity. He was a vicious brute, and so quick with his heels that it was a matter of some difficulty to handle him, and Archie was the only one who cared to attempt it. The wild horses seemed to miss him. They frequently came about the camp and called to him, and at such times he struggled so desperately to escape that the boys were alarmed lest he should injure himself.

Early on the morning following their arrival in the valley, they packed their bundles and took to their saddles for the return journey, Eugene leading Archie's old horse, and Archie himself riding the bay. They now had a good view of the gorge, and it was so full of obstructions—tangled thickets, fallen trees and boulders that had tumbled from the cliffs above—and the path was so narrow and winding, that it was a mystery to them how the horses could have found their way through there in the dark. They stopped once for a short rest and lunch, and about three o'clock in the afternoon arrived within sight of the prairie. They thought of the wild man, but saw no signs of him.

The way was now clear, and being impatient to reach the Fort and exhibit their prize, they put their horses into a lope, and by the time the sun began to dip behind the mountains they had made fifteen miles farther on their journey. They followed a course a few miles to the eastward of the route they had first travelled, in order to find water. They knew just where to look for it, for the trapper had been very explicit in his instructions, and Eugene had communicated them to his companions while they were yet fresh in his memory, so that there might be no chance for any mistakes. The willows, which pointed out the position of the stream, came in sight at last, and then the boys halted and held a consultation. A thin cloud of smoke slowly rising above the tops of the trees showed them that their camping-ground was already occupied.

"Ask me something hard," said Archie, when his companions, after looking at the smoke through their field-glasses, turned to him as if to inquire what he thought about it. "I am sure I don't know who they are."

"What shall we do?" asked Fred. "I don't like the idea of going into a stranger's camp, for I have not forgotten Frank's experience with Black Bill and his party."

"But Dick assured me that we had nothing to fear from any one we might meet," said Eugene. "He told me, too, that if we got into any difficulty 'he and old Bob would be around."

"Perhaps Dick and Bob are there now," said Archie.

"That's so. We can go down and see, and if they are strangers we need not intrude upon them. We can go a mile or two farther up the stream."

The boys rode down the swell, and in a few minutes reached the willows that lined both banks of the stream. No sooner had they entered them than a chorus of angry yelps and growls arose in advance, and three or four gaunt, savage-looking hounds came toward them with open mouths.

"Begone, you brutes!" shouted a voice. "Begone, I say! Come on, strangers, whoever you be. They won't pester you."

The boys kept on, and when they reached the other side of the willows, came in sight of the camp. Two covered wagons were drawn up, one on each side of the fire, and a span of small, shaggy mules and a yoke of very poor oxen were grazing close by on the prairie. About the fire were gathered a party of men, women and children, half a score in number, all but two of whom the boys at once put down as emigrants. Three of these emigrants were men—one an old gray-headed patriarch, and the others sturdy young fellows, one of whom must have been some relation to the old man, if there was any faith to be put in the resemblance they bore to each other.

The two who were not emigrants reminded the

boys of that brace of worthies who had ridden into
their camp on the night Walter was spirited away—
Parks and Reed—who were now safe in irons in the
Fort.   The dress and accoutrements of these men
proclaimed them to be hunters, but their faces told
a different story.   They did not seem at all pleased
to see the boys, but the old man welcomed him
cordially.

"How do, strangers?" said he. "Alight and
hitch."

"We're obliged to you," said Archie, "but we
have no wish to intrude. We thought, when we
saw the smoke of your fire, that perhaps we should
find some of our friends here. We'll make our
camp a little farther up the stream."

"No intrusion at all," said the old man. "You
are almost the only white folks we've seen for weeks
till we fell in with our friends here——" nodding
his head toward the two hunters—"and we'd like to
talk to you."

Archie hesitated. If the old man wanted him
and his companions to camp with him, it was plain

that the hunters did not, and he was well enough acquainted with men of their class to know that it was sometimes a dangerous proceeding to act in opposition to their wishes. But then these men did not belong to the train. Archie judged by what the old man said that he and his company had fallen in with them accidentally during their journey across the prairie, and if that was the case, they had nothing to say.

"Better get down," urged the emigrant. "We've got grub enough to feed you. We're on our way to Fort Bolton; where might you be a travellin' to ?"

" We're bound for the same place."

"Then camp with us to-night and to-morrow we'll travel in company."

The promise of a good supper was a very tempting one to the hungry boys, whose commissary would have been exhausted long ago if they had given their appetites full swing, and they knew that if they accepted the emigrant's invitation their wants would be abundantly supplied. There was a coffee-

pot on the coals, something that looked like biscuits
in a pan beside the fire, and from one of the trees
hung a joint of fresh meat, from which had been cut
a sufficient number of steaks to fill a large frying-
pan. The fact that the tin plates and cups that
were scattered around were not as clean as some
they had seen, and that the emigrant's wife went
about her domestic duties with a pipe in her mouth,
did not take the sharp edge off their appetites, as it
might have done a few months before. So they
decided to remain. The old man took their bundles,
accompanied them when they went out to picket
their horses, asked them more questions than he
would give them time to answer, and finally went
back to camp to make sure that his wife had obeyed
orders and added more steaks to those already in
the pan.

Fred and Eugene, having picketed their own
horses, went to assist Archie, the bay having suddenly taken it into his head that he would not allow
himself to be staked out. The boys had a lively

battle with him, and while it was going on, one of the hunters came out.

"Look a yer! who be you an' what brought you yer?" he demanded.

Archie, who had quite as much on his hands as he could attend to, was not in just the right mood to answer such questions, especially when propounded, as this one was, with all the insolence the man could throw into his tones. He paid no attention to it until the man said, pointing his finger at him:

"You heard me, I reckon! What's your name, an' what brought you yer?"

"There, he's safe enough," said· Fred, when he had driven down the iron picket-pin with the hatchet.

"We'll not trust to that alone," said Archie. "We'll hobble him, too. Now, my friend, in reply to your question I have to say that I left all my cards at 'Frisco; but when I return there, as I expect to do in the course of a month or so, I will send you one, if you will be kind enough to give me your address."

The man stared, and then looked down at the ground in a brown study. He could not make head or tail of what Archie said; but when Eugene spoke, he began to have a vague idea that the boys were making game of him.

"We'll send it by special train, too," said Eugene, who was highly indignant over the man's insulting manner.

"I don't want no sass," said the latter. "I axed you a fair question."

"But you didn't ask it in a fair way," said Archie. "Now, then, stand clear of his heels and I will let him go," he added, as Eugene buckled the halter-strap around the bay's leg below his knee. "I think we shall find him here when we want him."

The horse was doubly secured now. He was fastened by a lariat to an iron pin, which was driven as deeply into the ground as repeated blows from the hatchet could send it, and his head was tied down to his feet, so that even if he succeeded in pulling the pin out he could not run away. The boys had found that these precautions were absolutely necessary. They had been so long about this work that the fresh steaks had had plenty of time to cook, and when they went back to camp the host told them that supper was ready, and backed up his welcome announcement by grasping the frying-pan by its long handle and passing it to each of his guests in succession, who helped themselves by using their hunting-knives in lieu of forks. The host, not being so particular, fished his share out with his fingers. The emigrant's wife passed them each a biscuit with a hand which looked as though it had never seen water; a tin cup, with which one of the youngsters had been amusing himself, was filled with coffee and handed over with the remark: "I reckon you three haint afeared of one another;" and everything being thus satisfactorily arranged and everybody provided for, the host found a seat and applied himself to the task of learning a full history of everything our heroes had done since they were born. After asking a few questions he suddenly paused, having thought of something.

"I declare, I'm losin' all my manners since I left the settlements," said he. "I'm Reuben Holmes, gentlemen, all the way from Pike, Missouri. That chap there," he added, pointing to one of the young men, "he's Reuben Holmes, junior. He's my son. Know him, strangers."

The boys, with great difficulty controlling their desire to laugh, bowed to Reuben Holmes, junior, who did not know enough to acknowledge it in any way, and the old man went on.

"This 'yer's my old woman; that big gal is my darter, and them's my young children. That chap is Simon Cool, my hired help. He's going out to the mines to run a quartz-mill for me. Them two," waving a biscuit toward the two hunters, "are Zack and Sile. I don't know their other names, but they're friends of our'n. They met us on the prairie, and finding that we were a trifle out of our reckoning, they took us in tow and are going to show us the way to where we want to go. We're bound for the mines, and I am going to set up a quartz-mill there."

Having thus, as he imagined, placed our heroes quite at their ease, the old man took a bite out of his biscuit, first dipping it into the frying-pan, and went on with his questioning. The boys good-naturedly replied, paying no heed to the winks, nods and grunts of disbelief which the two hunters constantly exchanged with Simon Cool, and finally the emigrant came down to their recent exploits.

"Where you been lately and what a doing?" he asked.

"We have just come from the mountains," was the reply of Archie, who acted as spokesman.

"Humph!" grunted Zack.

"What were you doing there?"

"Hunting wild horses."

"Did you ever hear tell of the like of that, Zack?" asked Silas.

"I never did," was the answer. "They're nice lookin' chaps to go a huntin' wild hosses, haint they now?"

"An' the mountains is a likely place to find 'em, too," added Silas.

"Is that frisky critter of your'n out there a wild hoss?" asked the old man.

"He is."

"Well, I do think in my soul! And you did ketch him, didn't you? You say you're going to Bolton to-morrow?"

"Yes."

"How far is it from here?"

"About three days' journey, the way you will travel. We, on horseback, could accomplish it in less time."

"Which way is it from here?"

"Off there."

"Why how does that come?" said the emigrant, with some surprise. "We've been travelling *that* way for the last two days," pointing in just the opposite direction.

"Then you have lost your course, or else somebody has been misleading you."

"Don't listen to 'em, old man," said Zack. "Tain't noways likely that me an' Sile could get lost."

"We don't suppose you could," said Eugene, who had been made so angry by the hunters' sly winks and nods that he could scarcely restrain himself. "You know where the Fort is as well as we do."

"I reckon we do, an' better," said Zack.

Simon Cool, for some reason or other, had been making persevering, but unavailable, efforts to turn the conversation into another channel, and Archie, seeing that Eugene was treading on dangerous ground, joined in with Simon, and finally succeeded in getting the old man started on the subject of mining, on which he could talk like a book. Archie listened until he had finished his supper, and then went out to look at his horse. He glanced over his shoulder as he went, and saw that Simon and the two hunters were sitting with their heads close together, as if engaged in consultation.

"There's something afoot," thought Archie, "and I have half a mind to saddle up and clear out. Here comes Eugene. I'll see what he thinks about it."

CHAPTER IX.

AN ENEMY IN CAMP.

I HEARD Dick talking about Pikes the other day," said Eugene, who had followed Archie in order to lend his assistance in case the bay had succeeded in freeing himself from his halter or lariat. "Did he refer to such people as our friends here?"

"He did," answered Archie. "As I understand it, these Pikes are one of the results of our late war. A good many of the people in the border states were completely broken up, their houses being burned, their crops destroyed and their stock killed or driven off. It takes time and patience to accumulate property by farming, and it is hard for a man to begin over again where he began twenty or forty years ago. There are not many who have the courage to do it. These people had heard wonderful stories of the mines and the sudden fortunes sometimes made there, and believing that since they had to dig in the ground for a living, it would be easier to dig gold and silver than potatoes, they emigrated by regiments. But where one family made a permanent settlement in California, a dozen turned back. But still some of them were not satisfied, and after staying a year or two in their old homes, they would bundle up again and go back to California; and from roaming about so much, they fell into the habit of leading a wandering, gipsy life. They are not satisfied with a permanent settlement anywhere. How the name they bear came to be applied to them I don't know, unless it was because the first of them came from Pike county, Missouri. This man is a genuine Pike. There is no telling how many times he has wandered back and forth over these prairies, but he hasn't learned much during his wanderings. I have crossed the prairie only once, and I know that he is a hundred miles north of where he belongs."

"Well, now, hasn't it occurred to you—" said Eugene, looking over his shoulder to make sure that there was no one listening; "by the way, what do you think of them, any how?"

"I think there is one crazy man in that party, and two, and perhaps three, villains."

Eugene reached out his hand and gave Archie an approving slap on the back, as if to say that he had given utterance to his own ideas on that point.

"The old man talks sensibly enough about some things," said he, "but he is wild on the subject of money, and has an eye that you don't see belonging to a person whose head is perfectly level. Now hasn't it struck you——"

"That those two hunters are leading him out of his way for some purpose of their own?" added Archie, when Eugene paused. "It has, and I believe it."

"But what is their object?"

"You tell. There's nothing in those wagons worth stealing, I am sure. Hold on; here comes one of them."

Simon Cool was approaching. When he came up he stated his business without ceremony.

" Look a yer, strangers," said he, turning his head on one side and squirting at Archie, " I want to know what brought you yer."

" We have already told you," answered Archie. " We expected to find some of our friends here."

" Wal, seein' you didn't find 'em, hadn't you better toddle on ?"

" I don't know. What do you think about it ?"

" I reckon as how you had. Zack and Sile don't like the idea of your hangin' around. They say you're here for no good."

" They're judging us by themselves; but we'll go. We've no desire to stay where we are not wanted. Let's get our bundles, Eugene. We can saddle our horses out here without taking them to the camp."

" Where you going?" demanded the Pike, as the boys entered the camp, and after giving Fred a nod which he understood, began gathering up their property. " Going further ?"

" Yes, we thought we would ride on," replied Archie. " We can make a mile or two before dark, and that will take us just that much nearer the Fort."

"I hate to have you go, 'cause we might travel in company in the morning. If you happen around this way agin, drop in," said the Pike, repeating the stereotyped invitation he had often extended to his neighbors at home.

"Thank you," said Fred. "We are indebted to you and your good lady for your hospitality, and hope we shall have a chance to reciprocate."

"Which?" exclaimed the Pike.

"We thank you for the good supper you have given us," said Archie.

"No occasion, strangers; no occasion. Call often. We always leave the latch-string hanging out, and keep a bite for anybody that's hungry."

The boys bade the hospitable Pike good-by, shouldered their bundles and saddles and left the camp. An hour afterward they were safely settled in a camp of their own about three miles further up the stream. Of course they had plenty to talk about during the evening, the family they had just left and the misfortunes that would most likely befall them, if they trusted themselves to the guidance of the two hunters, forming the principal topics of the conversation. At eleven o'clock the horses were brought in and tied in the edge of the willows, and Archie and Eugene wrapped themselves in their blankets and went to sleep, while Fred sat up to keep an eye on the bay, and see that Zack and Silas did not steal a march on them during the night.

Morning came at length, and after the boys had drank the last of their coffee—they had scarcely enough of the article left to make the hot water taste like coffee—and eaten their last piece of cracker, they made up their bundles and prepared to resume their journey. It was high time, they told one another, that something was done in the way of hunting. They had seen no game when they passed over the ground a few days before, and unless some stray antelope or buffalo put itself in their way, they would be obliged to go supperless to bed.

The bay behaved so badly on this particular

morning that Archie found it impossible to bridle him, so he made a bridle out of his lasso, passing the bight over the horse's head behind his ears, through his mouth, tying it firmly under his lower jaw, and leading the ends over his neck and around the horn of his saddle to serve as reins. Their preparations being completed they mounted and set off at a gallop, and the first living objects they saw when they reached the top of the nearest swell were the emigrant and his family, who were following a course lying at right angles with their own.

"Good-morning to you," cried the old man, who was marching beside one of the wagons. "Off for the Fort now?"

"Yes, sir," replied the boys.

"Heading the wrong way, haint you?"

"No, sir; we're heading directly toward it."

"I say," exclaimed the emigrant suddenly, "you're——"

When he had said this, the two hunters and Simon began to remonstrate with him. The boys could not catch their words, but they distinctly heard the old man say: "Do you want me to let them youngsters go off and lose themselves? It is my bounded duty to set 'em right."

"I say," shouted the old man again, "you'll never see Bolton if you go that way. You're going wrong. Zack and Sile say we'll be there to-night?"

"Well, Zack and Sile know better than that. You are the one who is going wrong. We know what we are talking about, when we assure you that you are heading as straight from the Fort as you can go!"

"Whoa!" shouted the Pike, bringing both his teams to a stand still. "This thing must be settled now. Come here, boys."

The three friends moved toward the wagon, but Archie's horse declining to approach very near, pretending to be much afraid of the white canvas covers, his rider was obliged to dismount and lead him.

"Now if the Fort is off there, as you say it is,

what is the reason that Zack and Sile are leading us the other way?" demanded the Pike.

" They have reasons of their own, with which we are not acquainted," answered Archie. " But they are going to lose you, and they know it."

Silas made an angry rejoinder, and this was the beginning of the conversation which we have already recorded. We have related all that passed during the interview, and told how the Pike, suddenly becoming impressed by Archie's statements, abruptly abandoned the guides he had so long followed, and placed himself and family under the directions of the boys. We have also told of the astounding revelation he afterward made in regard to the treasure which one of his vehicles contained, the manner in which it was received by the three friends, and the discussion on the weight of money that followed, when the old man left them and drew back beside his wagon. We are now ready to take up our story where we left off.

"I know now why Zack and Silas were so anxious to be rid of us," said Archie. "They have designs on that money, or whatever it is, and wanted a clear field for their operations."

"And don't you think Simon Cool is somehow mixed up with them?" asked Featherweight. "He seemed to be on pretty good terms with them."

"*I* thought so," said Eugene; "but it seems to me that if he were in league with them, he would have gone off with them, instead of staying with the train."

"Unless he can serve his purpose and theirs better by remaining," said Archie, significantly.

"I didn't think of that."

"Well, their plans, if they had any, are knocked higher than a kite," said Fred, "and all we have to do is to keep our eyes open. I, for one, am glad things turned out as they have, for now we are sure of something to eat without the trouble of hunting for it. But, fellows, I'd like to know what's in that wagon. Wouldn't it be a good plan to question the Pike, as he questioned us last night?"

During that forenoon the boys were left entirely to themselves. The emigrant remained close beside his wagon, and once when the boys looked at him they found that he had put on his powder-horn, and bullet-pouch, and that he carried his long rifle on his shoulder. He kept looking back, too, as if he feared the hunters might follow the train; but they were not once seen during the day.

When the wagons halted at noon the Pike had but little to say to the boys, and that little related entirely to the conversation that had taken place that morning—the location of the Fort, the distance they must travel before reaching it, and the probable object that Zack and Silas had in view in trying to mislead him. He had not yet recovered from his fright. During the halt he visited the wagon every few minutes, pulled up the cover and looked under it to satisfy himself that his valuables were safe; but he always took care to fasten the cover down again, so that the boys, although they passed the wagon a dozen times, on some pretext or other, could not obtain a glimpse of the interior. When they stopped for the night his vigilance seemed to increase. After supper he made the circuit of the camp several times, with his rifle in his hand, and having satisfied himself that there were no enemies near, he spread his blanket under the wagon and went to sleep.

The boys brought their horses in at an early hour and also sought their blankets. They had been almost constantly in the saddle during the last five days, and began to feel the effects of their long journey. It had been their custom, while they were alone on the prairie, to set a watch every night, but now there seemed to be no need of it. The only thing they feared was that the bay might find means to escape; but he seemed to be pretty well contented just now, and he was as secure as two raw-hide ropes could make him. If a stranger approached the camp, he would be the first to hear him. And then, there were the dogs! All the emigrants seemed to put unbounded faith in them, and if the Pike was willing to trust himself and his property to their watchfulness, the boys thought they would run no risk in doing the same. They agreed among themselves, however, that each one should sleep with both ears open, and be ready to jump up the instant he heard any unusual sounds.

All the emigrants were locked in slumber long before the boys laid down, at least they appeared to be; but there was one who was wide awake, and waiting with a little impatience for them to stop talking and go to sleep. It was the teamster, Simon Cool. He waited half an hour, and then slowly and cautiously raised his head and looked about him. He glanced sharply at each one of the prostrate forms, and quietly threw off his blanket. Having arranged it so that a casual glance at it would lead one to suppose that it still covered a human figure, he pulled off his heavy boots and slipped away barefooted in the darkness.

He was gone a long time, and when he returned and entered the camp, he did it with so much cau- tion that no one heard him. He did not even attract the attention of the bay. The dogs looked at him, but they had known him so long that he had nothing to fear from them. He made his way on his hands and knees to the place where the boys lay, side by side, and quickly, but without the least noise, removed their rifles and the belts containing their revolvers, which they had placed at the head of their beds. This done, he looked toward young Reuben Holmes, but it was only to see if he was still asleep; for Simon knew that he had nothing about him more dangerous than a rusty pocket-knife, and that was not worth securing. The only weapon belonging to the Holmes family was the heavy, old-fashioned rifle which the old man had taken to bed with him. This Simon secured as easily as he had secured the rest, and taking them all in his arms carried them out of the camp and laid them on the ground, placing Archie's Maynard and a brace of the revolvers by themselves. He had disarmed everybody in the camp in less than two minutes' time, and they all slept on unconscious of it.

CHAPTER X.

THE PIKE'S TREASURE.

HAVING performed his work of disarming the camp, in a manner perfectly satisfactory to himself, Simon Cool crawled back to his bed, drew on his boots and crept under his blanket again. Scarcely was he fairly settled when two figures arose from the ground, about two hundred yards from the camp, where they had been lying watching all his movements, and ran forward to the place where he had deposited the weapons. They threw down their own rifles, quickly buckled a brace of revolvers about their waists and took possession of the sixteen-shooters belonging to Fred and Eugene. Their own rifles and the emigrant's they hid away in the willows, and then boldly approached the camp. The sound of their footsteps aroused the horse and dogs, and these in turn aroused the slumbering men and boys, who started up to see Zack and Silas standing before the fire with the stolen weapons in their hands. There was not one among them who displayed half as much terror and astonishment at this unwelcome sight as did Simon Cool.

"Keep quiet now an' do as you're told, an' thar shan't a har of your heads be hurted," said Zack. "But if anybody goes to raisin' a rumpus he'll allers be sorry fur it, 'cause he won't live as long as it 'd take a hoss to jerk his tail twice."

For a few seconds no one moved or spoke. They had all been awakened out of a sound sleep, and it required a little time and effort for them to gather their wits about them. The boys did not fully understand the words that had been addressed to them, but the simple presence of the two hunters was all that was needed to explain matters to them.

The Pike was utterly bewildered at first, but gradually he began to comprehend the situation; and when he had fully grasped it, his terror knew no bounds. Jumping from his blanket before either of the hunters could prevent him, he spread out his arms before the wagon which contained his treasure, and broke out into wild lamentations and defiance.

"I know what you're here for," he cried, "but you shan't have it. You *can't* have it, for it's robbery, and that's something the law don't allow. I'll have you both in jail if you touch it. I've spent years on it and worked hard for it, and you shan't have it. I'll fight till I drop; so I will!"

The old man continued in this strain to give vent to his feelings of excitement and alarm, but the boys did not hear what else he said, for his wife, who had been looking on from the wagon in which she and the children slept, now joined in with her shrill voice, and a terrific uproar arose. Threats and the sight of the cocked rifles pointed full at their heads, at first had no effect on them. Their treasure was uppermost in their mind, and while that was in danger, they cared not for any peril that menaced themselves. After repeated efforts Zack succeeded in making himself heard and understood.

"We haint agoin' to harm none on you if we can

help it," said he; "but if you don't shut up, we'll tie yer hand and foot; and if that don't do you no good, we'll leave you yer to the wolves."

This threat restored silence. The Pike's wife drew her head back under cover of the wagon, and the old man wrung his hands and moaned to himself. In their heartfelt sympathy for him, the boys, for the time, forgot that they were prisoners themselves.

"Now, if you've come to yer senses, we'll be movin'," said Zack. "You two," nodding to Reuben and Simon, "hitch up the oxen an' mules, an' you, Sile, saddle a horse for me an' you an' turn the rest loose!'

These orders showed that there was a journey before them, and so the boys, at Archie's suggestion, began making up their bundles, keeping their eyes on Silas all the while, to see which of their horses he was going to saddle. His first thought evidently was to take the bay; but the horse turned his heels toward him, laid back his ears and looked so savage, that Silas changed his mind, and making a wide circuit around him to get at his head, he drew his knife across the lariats with which he was confined, and set him at liberty.   With a joyful neigh the bay kicked up his heels and galloped off, the ends of the lariats streaming in the air behind him.   The boys saw it all, but did not speak until they had made up their bundles and thrown them into one of the wagons.   Like the man who went twenty miles after a load of sand, and when he reached home, found that his wagon was as empty as when he started, the sand having all leaked out through the cracks, they felt that their knowledge of the English language would not enable them to do the subject justice, so they kept still for a while and thought about it.

"There are five days' work gone to the bow-wows," sighed Archie, at length.

"And Frank Nelson, with his black, is still ahead of the hounds," murmured Featherweight.

"I would be willing to remain a prisoner six months, if the bay had only given Silas one good kick before he left," said Eugene, savagely. "What shall we say when we get back to the Fort—if we ever do?"

" We'll say that we caught the horse," said Archie, with an attempt to appear cheerful, " but that circumstances over which we had no control prevented us from keeping him."

" Humph!" exclaimed Eugene. " It is just too provoking for anything."

" But it can't be helped," said Fred, " and we might as well laugh as cry over it."

" Throw us a couple of saddles yer," said Silas, who at this moment came up, leading Archie's horse and Eugene's.

" What have you done with my nag?" asked Fred.

" Turned him loose, I reckon," was the encouraging reply. " I turned two loose."

" Then I might as well put my saddle away in the bushes,' said Fred, " so that I shall know where to find it if I ever have occasion to use it again."

When the preparations for their journey were all completed, Reuben and Simon, in obedience to orders, climbed to their seats in the wagons and drove after Zack, who rode over the prairie ; the boys and the Pike fell in behind on foot, and Silas brought up the rear, riding Archie's horse and carrying one of the Henry rifles across the horn of his saddle.

" I declare this beats anything I ever heard of," said Eugene, whose wrath had not yet had time to cool ; " six able-bodied fellows captured and marched off by one-third of their number !"

" But it isn't so very bad after all, when you come to think of it," returned Fred. " I have heard of three car-loads of passengers being robbed by four men."

" These hunters must have followed us all day yesterday," continued Eugene, " and of course they are after the Pike's money ; but I don't see how they could have come into our camp and taken possession of our weapons without awakening some of us."

" Ask them how they did it," suggested Archie. " They know."

Acting on the hint, Eugene turned to Silas, who

was riding close behind them, and propounded the question to him; but that worthy only shook his head and grinned, and that was all they could get out of him. Eugene persisted until his two companions expected to see the hunter become angry; but he did not. He was in a very good humor, and no doubt the prospect of soon handling a million dollars was what made him so. The old man was depressed in the same degree that Silas was elated. The first burst of grief being over, he had nothing to say, but his whole frame quivered and his face was convulsed with agony.

The boys were not at all alarmed at their situation—they were only angry and sorry; angry because the horse for which they had worked so hard had been taken from them, and sorry for the Pike, who was about to be deprived of his hard-earned wealth. It was true that Eugene, as soon as his feelings of resentment had had time to wear away, began to be somewhat anxious in regard to that which was in store for them, but Archie quieted his fears by telling him just what was going to happen; and everything turned out as he said it would, except in one particular. They would be taken to some secluded place in the mountains, he said, so that they would be out of sight of anybody that might happen to pass on the prairie ; the wagons would be robbed of whatever articles of value they might contain, and they would then be at liberty to resume their journey. Their arrival at the Fort would not be delayed more than three or four days, at the very furthest.

"No plottin' agin the Dutch thar !" exclaimed Silas, noticing that the boys' heads were pretty close together, and that they were talking in low tones. "If you've got anything to say, speak it out, so't we can all hear it."

"Well, then, I'll ask you a question," said Archie. "What are you going to do with us ?"

"Nothing, if you behave yourselves," was the reply.

"Then why do you compel us to go with you so far out of our way? You've got all we have that is worth stealing."

"But you know too much. You might go back to the Fort an' make trouble for us," said Silas.

"You're right," said Archie, in a low tone, "and we may do it yet."

"You've got nobody to thank but yourselves," continued Silas. "Why didn't you cl'ar out, like we told you to, an' go about your business? If you'd a done it you'd a saved yourselves this trouble."

The long hours of the night dragged away wearily enough. Zack pushed ahead at a rapid walk, and the boys being more accustomed to their saddles than travelling on foot, soon became very tired. Dark as it was they managed to keep their bearings, and they knew that Zack was holding straight for the mountains. There was no halt ordered until they reached the foot-hills, and that was just as the day began to dawn. The wagons were driven into the willows out of sight, and the emigrant's wife, who had not once left her wagon, was instructed to "crawl out and dish up some grub!" an order which she obeyed with a very bad grace. During the meal but little was said by either captors or prisoners, and as soon as it was over the boys took their bundles from the wagon, spread out their blankets, and fell fast asleep almost as soon as they touched them. When they awoke the sun was setting, the emigrant's wife was preparing supper, and Reuben and Simon, acting under the directions of Silas, who kept guard over them with his rifle, were hitching up the mules and yoking the oxen preparatory to another start, which was made as soon as the supper was disposed of.

This night's journey was longer and harder than the preceding one, for it was begun at an earlier hour. The boys were not allowed to ride in the wagons, for Silas said they were slippery fellows— he knew it by the glint in their eyes—and he wanted them where he could watch them all the time.

Zack held along the base of the mountains, and at daylight our heroes found themselves travelling over ground that was familiar to them. The gully through which they had passed a few days before, and which led to the valley where the wild horse was captured, was close before them. Being almost ready to drop with fatigue they protested that it was quite impossible for them to go any farther, but Zack did not listen, for he was not yet ready to order a halt. He followed the gully as far as the rocks and fallen trees would allow him to go with the wagons, then turned into another and finally into a third, which was so much worse than any of the rest that, before they had gone a quarter of a mile, one of the wagons, having been shaken nearly to pieces by being hauled over boulders and logs, gave out entirely and came down with a crash.

"Thar', now, I reckon we'll stop," said Zack; and this was welcome news to the boys, who pulled their bundles out of the wagon and threw themselves upon them, completely tired out. But they quickly straightened up again and began to take some interest in what was going on, when they found that the trappers themselves did not intend to make a camp there. The two men held a short consultation, and some words which came to the boys' ears told them that the object of the undertaking was now about to be realized. The emigrant's wealth was to be brought to light.

"This is as good a place as any," said Silas. "They can't mend the wagon an' find their way out afore to-morrow, an' by that time we'll be miles away."

The expression on the emigrant's face showed that he too had overheard the words, and that he understood them, but he made no other sign. He had scarcely spoken for the last twenty-four hours. He seemed to be bewildered, stunned by his misfortunes. When Zack and Silas dismounted and raised the cover of the wagon which contained his treasure, he looked on in a stupid, benumbed sort of way, which almost led the boys to believe that he had taken leave of his senses.

"This must be it," said Silas, after taking a survey of the interior of the wagon. "It's the only thing yer that looks like a chist!"

The hunter thrust his hands into the wagon, and when he drew them out again they were grasping the handles of a small black trunk, which, like all the rest of the Pike's furniture that the boys had seen, looked as though it might have made many a journey between Missouri and California, for it was in a very dilapidated condition. The leather was worn off in a dozen places and the lid was loosely held on by one hinge and a piece of rope.

"There goes the labor of a lifetime, and I am a ruined man," sighed the Pike, resting his elbows on his knees and gazing at the box as if fascinated.

"They've got hold of it, then," whispered Archie, who would willingly have given everything he possessed to have been able to defend the old man's property. "How I wish Dick and old Bob would come in here now. It isn't money, though. It is too light."

"Thousand dollar greenbacks, may be," said Fred, in the same low whisper.

"Or bonds, perhaps," suggested Eugene.

The hunter's face expressed great astonishment. He had expected to find the trunk very heavy, but he lifted it with all ease with one hand. He had overheard the old man's words, however, and dashed at the box like a hound on a fresh trail. So great was his eagerness and impatience to see the inside of it, that his hands trembled with such violence that he could not undo the rope. The longer he tried the more the knot was jammed; and at last Zack, fully as impatient as his companion, whipped out his knife, cut the rope, and with one savage kick sent the lid flying into the air.

The old man groaned and the boys arose to their feet to obtain a view of the contents of the box. They could see no money or packages that might contain money or other valuables—nothing but a small brass frame, the inside of which was filled with wheels and weights made of the same material, the whole contrivance somewhat resembling the works of a clock. Silas stared at it a moment and then jerked it out of the box and threw it on the ground behind him, expecting no doubt to find something hidden under it. But this was all. The hunter then picked up the trunk, shook it, looked at it all over, thumped it with his knuckles, and

then to make sure that it contained no secret compartments, dashed it in pieces on the ground and
carefully examined each separate fragment.   He
was astounded, and so were the boys, who were looking on with almost breathless interest.

"Whar is it, old man?" panted Silas, scarcely
able to speak, so great was his excitement.

"Why there it is," said the Pike, gazing ruefully
at his machine, and then at the ruins of his trunk.
"There's uncounted millions in it!"

"In that?" shouted Silas.   "Whar's the
money?"

"I have no money.   That is yet to be earned."

A long silence followed this reply.   The expression of rage and disappointment on the hunters'
faces was curious to behold.

CHAPTER XI.

SNOWED UP.

I never in my life was so overjoyed to see men disappointed," whispered Eugene. " They've had all their trouble for nothing, and I am glad of it."

" Be careful," replied Archie, earnestly. " Don't say that again; for if they should chance to overhear you I don't know what they would do. They are perfectly desperate."

For two or three minutes the hunters stood like statues looking at one another, and then they made the cliffs echo with horrible yells and imprecations. Their rage was perfectly ungovernable and the boys trembled in fear of the result. Zack's first move was to demolish the machine, which he did most completely with one kick of his foot, sending the wheels and weights in every direction. Then he and Silas jumped into the wagons, which they proceeded to overhaul most thoroughly. Not the smallest article escaped close examination. Clothes were ripped up, in the hope of finding something hidden away in the seams; the one bed the family possessed was torn open and its contents scattered far and wide; skillets and frying-pans were sounded, as if the hunters expected to find some hidden compartments in them, and then smashed into atoms on the boulders; and in five minutes' time the emigrant had not a single whole article of furniture, bedding or clothing left. The boys looked on with great indignation, but were powerless to stop the wanton destruction. It would have been dangerous even to remonstrate with the enraged men.

"I say, fellows, just cast your eyes toward Simon," whispered Archie, suddenly.

The boys looked, and told themselves that some things which they had not been able to understand, were perfectly clear to them now. They had discovered another guilty man, and one whom nobody had suspected. If Simon Cool was not as much interested in finding the treasure as the hunters were, and if he was not as keenly disappointed to learn that the contents of the black trunk which the old man had watched so closely, were an invention of some kind, instead of a million dollars in gold, his face belied him.

"Do you know now how we were disarmed that night?" whispered Archie.

"I believe I do," replied Fred, "and I shouldn't wonder if the scamp was about to get himself into trouble. I certainly hope so. See how Zack and Silas scowl at him."

"If I thought you had fooled us a purpose, Simon, you'd never fool nobody else, I bet you," said Zack, in savage tones.

Simon glanced around with a frightened look, and saw that everybody had heard what the hunter said to him. Even the old man raised his head and listened.

"O, you needn't try to play off on us that way," exclaimed Silas, "You're as deep in the mud as we are, every bit. You told us that the ole man was wuth a million dollars—an' he's the lad who stole your we'pons from you while you was asleep," he added, nodding to our heroes.

"We thought so," answered Archie.

"Now if thar's any yaller boys about here, whar are they?" demanded Zack.

"I don't know," replied Simon, who saw that he could not conceal his real character any longer. "Everything the ole man's got was in that black chist. He told me so, an' said he wouldn't take a silver-mine fur it!"

The hunters looked keenly at Simon, and the expression on his face, rather than the words he had uttered, satisfied them that he had told the truth. The feelings of rage and disappointment which showed themselves in his countenance were genuine, and could not have been assumed.

"Wal, you an' the ole man atween you have got us into a scrape, an' we hain't made nothing by it," said Zack, at length. "Thar hain't none of us made nothing, I reckon," he added, glancing at the ruins of the Pike's furniture. "Now we want all

of you to stay here till we're safe out of the way ;
an' to make sure of your stayin'——"

Here Zack raised his rifle and shot one of the
oxen dead in the yoke. Silas shot the other and
then the mules, and thus the emigrant and his
family were left almost as helpless as they would
have been had they been cast away on some desert
island in the middle of the ocean. The hunters
then led their horses to the place where the boys
were standing, and Zack began untying his blankets,
which were fastened in a bundle behind his saddle.
Addressing himself to Archie, he said :

"A fair exchange hain't no robbery, they say, so
give me them blue ones o' yourn, an' I'll give you
mine. We hain't goin' away without something, I
bet you."

"I think you've got something already," said
Fred. "You've got a rifle worth forty-five dollars,
and a horse and saddle that cost almost a hundred
more."

"But we didn't get the million dollars, so hand
out them blankets!"

"An' I'll trade with *you*," said Silas, nodding to Fred.

Without another word of remonstrance the boys rolled up their clean, warm blankets, just as good now as the day they were purchased in San Francisco, in spite of the service they had seen, and handed them to the hunters, who gave them their own tattered and dirty army blankets in return. Although the boys could hardly bring themselves to touch them they did not refuse to take them, for they knew they would need them. The weather was cold, and it had been growing colder ever since they left the prairie. The wind came up the gorge in fitful gusts, whistling mournfully through the branches of the evergreens above their heads, and now and then the air was filled with flakes of snow. The storm which Dick Lewis had so confidently predicted had fairly set in, and some covering, besides the clothing they wore, was absolutely necessary.

"Now whar's the cartridges fur these we'pons?" said Silas.

11

"We haven't any," replied Fred and Eugene; and to prove it they turned their pockets inside out.

"Didn't you bring more'n one load with you?"

"One magazine full, you mean," said Eugene. "Isn't that enough? There were sixteen shots in one and fourteen in the other when we gave them to you—or rather when you took them. When those loads are gone you'll have to skirmish around and find more."

"An' whar's the ammunition fur these?" said Simon Cool, who now came up with a brace of revolvers buckled about his waist and carrying Archie's Maynard in his hands.

"Ah! you've got my rifle, have you?" said Archie. "I wondered what had become of it. There's a load in it, and much good may it do you. I haven't any more to give you."

It was perhaps fortunate for our heroes that the men did not ask any more questions about the ammunition. Fred and Eugene had thrown away their cartridges during the first night's march, declaring that if the hunters were going to steal their rifles, they needn't think they would get powder and bullets for nothing. Archie, however, who had not seen anything of his Maynard, and believed that it had been hidden somewhere near the camp, kept his cartridges; but when Zack and Silas over-hauled the wagons, his rifle was thrown out with the rest of the things, and then Archie pulled out his ammunition and dropped it behind the boulder on which he was sitting.

"You can't get anything to shoot in that rifle in this country," said Archie, " and since it is of no use to you, hadn't you better give it back to me? I have owned it a long time and don't like to part with it."

"I reckon I'll keep it," said Simon, in reply. " I reckon me an' my pardners can use it."

" Who's your pardners?" demanded Zack, quickly. "Not me an' Sile, I can tell you, fur you hain't goin' a step with us—not one step."

This showed that there had been some sort of an agreement between Simon and the hunters. No doubt when the million dollars were secured, they were to share it equally and travel in company.

"If you'll fool us once you'll do it agin; so we don't want nothing more to do with you," said Silas. "You can go your trail an' we'll go our'n."

"But I don't know whar to go," said Simon, who was utterly confounded; "an' I can't stay here."

"No, you can't stay here," said the old man. "When you were tramping about the country begging your living, I took you in and cared for you, and now you have turned against me! You can't stay here."

"This yer's a big country, an' thar's plenty of room in it fur all of us," said Zack.

With this piece of information the hunters mounted their horses and rode down the gully out of sight. Simon Cool stood motionless and silent for a moment, gazing fixedly at the ground, and then shouldering Archie's Maynard, he moved slowly away in the same direction and also disappeared. Bad as their situation was, the boys told themselves that Simon's was infinitely worse. They knew where to go to find friends and shelter; but Simon was turned adrift in a strange country, in the face of a blinding snow-storm, without a horse or blanket, and with only one load in his rifle to bring him subsistence. If that load failed him he would be in a predicament indeed, for his revolvers would be next to useless in hunting. They were intended only for short-range shooting, and such game as he would fall in with —if he was fortunate enough to fall in with any— would be wary and hard to approach, and could only be reached by a long-range rifle. It was at least one hundred and twenty-five miles to the Fort, and that was the nearest place at which Simon could procure food.

As soon as Simon was out of sight, Archie, who knew that there was nothing to be gained by sitting still and mourning over their hard fate, jumped to his feet and began to stir around. He set to work to gather up all the wheels and weights that had been scattered about when Zack demolished the machine that had been found in the trunk. His companions joined him in the search, and finally the Pike himself mustered up energy enough to lend his assistance.   His wife and son sat still and stared at the ruins of their furniture.

" Is this contrivance of yours, whatever it is, patented ?" asked Archie, who thought the old man might be induced to cheer up a little if he could be engaged in conversation.

" Not yet," was the answer.

" What do you intend to do with it ?"

" I was going to use it to run my quartz-mill."

" O, this is only a model, then !"

" Yes.   I accidentally found a rich gold-mine while I was in California, two years ago, but it could not be developed, because there was no power there to run a mill.   It would have cost a fortune to sink wells through the rock and bring a steam-engine over the mountains from Placer city ; but this invention of mine could have been put up in a week or ten days, and would have furnished power enough to run a dozen mills.   Just think of it !   I should have had that gold-mine all to myself, and there is no telling how rich it is.   Why, you can see the veins in the rock as thick as your finger. I am now sixty-five years old, and I have worked at this invention ever since I was twenty. I got it done just at the right time, too, and now I must lose all my work."

"Perhaps not. The machinery is all here, and can be put together again. It doesn't look as if it were damaged at all. What motive-power are you going to use—steam or water ?"

"Nary one. The invention furnishes its own power."

It was wonderful what a change these few words made in the boys' feelings towards the old man. The wheels and weights, which they had before handled so carefully, were bundled promiscuously together and thrown into one of the wagons. They had no more time to waste with the machine or with the inventor, either. A man who could squander forty-five years of the one life he had to live, in studying perpetual motion, was not just the sort of person they wanted to associate with in an emergency like the present.

"Let the machine go," whispered Eugene. "It isn't worth the trouble it has caused us. Let's tell the old fellow that we're going to start for the Fort, and that if he wants to go with us, he had better be getting ready."

Archie, who was always expected to speak for his companions, accordingly informed the Pike that it was high time they were making a move in some direction, unless they wanted to stay there and be snowed up; told him that he and his friends proposed making an immediate start for the Fort, and asked him if he wished to accompany them. The old man said he did, but he had no suggestions to make, and indeed seemed to take but little interest in the matter. He was too busy trying to put his machine together again. The boys, in great disgust, turned from him to his wife, who, as Featherweight afterward declared, was the only man in the family. The Pike himself was plainly crazy, and Reuben was as stupid as a block.

"Mrs. Holmes, we don't want to stay here and freeze," said Archie, "so we're going to try to reach Fort Bolton. We shall find friends there. It is a long journey to make on foot, but of course you would rather attempt it than stay here alone."

"In course I would," said the woman.

"Then I suggest that we cut up one of these oxen, and that you cook as much of the meat as we can carry. We'll build you a good fire, and while you are at work, we'll bundle up the best of these quilts and blankets, and put the rest of your baggage in the wagons. It will then be protected from the weather, and you will know where to find it in case you should ever want to come after it. But we have no time to waste. We ought to make at least eight or ten miles on our way before dark."

"You, Rube," exclaimed the woman, suddenly, "get up an' go to work. Your pop's machine is played out, our million dollars is up stump, an' we bein' poor people agin, you've got to scratch with the rest of us. Git up; you've been settin' thar like a lump on a log long enough."

These words seemed to put a little life into Reuben. He found a knife and went to work at one of the oxen; Fred and Archie gathered a supply of wood and started a fire; while Eugene employed himself in tying up the quilts and blankets. Everybody was busy except the old man, who was still wasting his time with his machine.

While the boys were at work they found opportunity, now and then, to glance up at the threatening clouds above them, and they shivered involuntarily and looked askance at one another when they thought of the long journey before them. It was evident that a furious storm was raging, although they did not feel it, being securely sheltered by the cliffs. But little snow fell where they were, the gale carrying it across the gorge above their heads; but when it came down to them, as it did now and then, when brought by an eddying wind, it fell in a blinding shower, and gave them some idea of what must be the state of affairs on the exposed prairie.

After two hours' hard work, Archie announced that they were ready to begin their journey. The Pike's wife had cooked a supply of meat sufficient to last three or four days, and they had also been able to save from the wreck enough corn-meal and flour to make about half a bushel of " slap-jacks," which had been baked before the fire on heated stones. Although the old man seemed to be very much interested in his work, he kept an eye on all that was going on, and when he saw that preparations for the start were being made, he packed his machine carefully away in a blanket which he had selected for the purpose, shouldered the bundle Archie pointed out to him and marched cheerfully off with the others. He began to act more like himself now. He had discovered that a few hours' work would make his machine just as good as it was before.

Archie, who was leading the way, had not gone many rods before he told himself that their attempt to reach the Fort was certain to prove a failure. He knew that the storm was a hard one, but he had only a faint idea of its fury until he had fairly left the shelter of the cliffs. In the first gully they entered the snow covered the ground to the depth of three or four inches, and in some

places had been whirled into drifts that reached
almost to the tops of his boots. The main
gully—the one that led to the valley in which the
wild horse had been captured—was even worse.
If the storm continued twenty-four hours longer,
it would be quite impassable. They kept bravely
on, carrying the crying children by turns and
shifting their heavy bundles from one shoulder
to the other, until they came within sight of the
prairie, and there they stopped. It was folly to
think of going farther.

Fred and Eugene were appalled at the sight
presented to their gaze, and Archie, who had
witnessed many a New England snow-storm, declared
that he had never seen anything like it. They
could not see twenty yards in any direction, except
down the gully from which they had just emerged.
Everything was concealed by the drifting snow.
The wind blew a gale, and the boys could not face
it for a moment. Fred and Eugene shielded their
eyes with their arms and looked at Archie to see
what he thought about it.

"I am afraid to try it," said the former. "The snow cuts like a knife. I never saw anything like this in Louisiana. I am so cold already that I can scarcely talk."

"We can't try it," said Archie; "it is out of the question. We could not go a quarter of a mile against this wind to save our lives. Besides, just as soon as we got out of sight of the mountains, which would be in less than two minutes, we should lose our way and that would be the last of us. We must go back and wait until the storm is over."

Upon hearing this decision, Fred and Eugene quickly retreated to the gully, where the Pike and his family had already taken refuge, while Archie followed more leisurely, glancing back at the prairie occasionally, looking up at the clouds, as if trying to judge of the probable duration of the storm, and then fastening his eyes on the ground, as if revolving some problem in his mind.

"We're snowed up," said he, when he joined his companions again. "I was afraid of it, but it is nothing we can help, so we must make the best of it.

We must go back to the wagons.   That is the most
sheltered spot I know of.   Hadn't you better go
ahead and build up the fire?" he added, turning to
the Pike, who was shaking like a man with the ague.
"Your children will perish if you keep them out
here.   We will follow you as soon as we leave something to guide our friends, who will be certain to
hunt us up in a few days."

CHAPTER XII.

THE SILENT WITNESS.

MEANWHILE Dick Lewis and those of the Club who remained at the Fort, were await-ing the return of the wanderers with no little im-patience. Dick, who knew almost to an hour how long they ought to be gone, exhibited no anxiety until the sixth day, and then he began to be uneasy. He made frequent trips to the summit of a high swell near the Fort, gazed long and earnestly in the direction the boys had gone, looked dubiously at the clouds, and was always moody and silent when he returned to the camp. On one occasion, when he had been on the lookout nearly all day, he was met by George Le Dell, who seemed to be greatly excited about something.

"What is it, youngster?" exclaimed the trapper.

"Your face says you've got news of some sort for me."

"Come with me and see for yourself," replied George. "I may be mistaken, and certainly hope I am. I haven't said a word about it, for I didn't want to excite any unnecessary alarm."

George, followed by the trapper, made a wide circuit around the camp, and entering the grove from the opposite side, walked into it a short distance, and then stopped and pointed to a horse which was hitched to one of the trees.

"I found him feeding with my horse, and brought him in here to keep him until you came," said George. "I hope I have made a mistake."

"Wal, you hain't," said the trapper, bluntly. "That's leetle Fred's hoss, if I ever seed him. Something's happened to them keerless fellers."

"That's what I was afraid of," said George, an expression of anxiety settling on his face. "You see he has a piece of rawhide rope around his neck. He never broke that."

"In course he didn't," said the trapper. "I've

a notion to tell ole Bob to give me a good wallopin' fur lettin' 'em go. The snow'll be four foot deep afore this time to-morrow, an' something's got to be done, right quick."

As the trapper spoke he untied the horse and led him through the grove to the camp. Uncle Dick and all the boys were there, and, as may be imagined, the trapper's appearance created no little commotion among them. They recognised Fred's horse at once.

" Thar hain't no need of wastin' time an' words over it," said Dick, hurriedly. " This hoss's lariat has been cut with a knife, an' he's come home. Fred didn't cut it himself, in course; so something's happened to them boys, an' me an' Bob's got to see about it, to onct. We'd oughter gone two days ago. I kinder felt it in my bones."

The Club and Uncle Dick said plainly enough by their actions that if the trappers were going to look for the missing boys, they were not going alone. A general rush was made for bridles, saddles and weapons, and confusion reigned supreme

until Uncle Dick took the management of affairs
into his own hands. Two of the boys were directed
to hitch the mules to the wagon, drive them up to
the Fort and request permission of the colonel to
leave them there until they should be called for;
another was instructed to strike the tent and pack
it away in the wagon; another to get out a supply
of bacon, hard-tack and coffee sufficient to last them
a week; and the two trappers to saddle the horses.
Uncle Dick himself bundled up the blankets; and
order being thus established, and each one having a certain duty to perform, everything was done
in a very short space of time.

Colonel Gaylord readily promised to take charge
of such of the Club's property as they wished to
leave behind, and took the trouble to come down to
camp to see what the matter was. When he had
heard Uncle Dick's story, he generously offered him
a squad of cavalry to assist in hunting up the boys,
but the trappers said they didn't need it.

In half an hour the whole party were in the saddle and the Fort was out of sight. Frank Nelson,

of course, led the way. He went at such a rate of speed that the foot-hills were reached a little after midnight, and there Dick Lewis ordered a halt. The storm was by this time fairly under way, and a terrible one it was, too. Walter and the rest of the boys from Louisiana, who had never experienced anything of the kind before, were amazed at its violence, and even Uncle Dick and the two trappers, who had "roughed it" all their lives, said it was something rather out of the ordinary. It continued all night, and the next morning the little hollows between the swells were filled with snow. The wind seemed to blow with redoubled force as the day advanced, but it was at their backs, and by keeping close along the edge of the hills, Uncle Dick and his party were in some measure protected from its fury. They were all warmly clad and suffered but little from the cold. They did not stop again until near the middle of the afternoon, and then a circumstance happened which gave the Club an opportunity to gain some idea of the wonderful skill in woodcraft possessed by their two backwoods companions.

Dick Lewis, who was riding by Frank's side, suddenly drew rein, turned his horse's head toward the willows which lined the base of the hills, and after snuffing the air a few times, looked inquiringly at old Bob. The latter nodded his head and Dick exclaimed: "It hain't fur off. We must go back."

"What isn't far off, and why must we go back?" asked George.

"I smell smoke," replied Dick.

The boys looked at one another a moment, but none of them could understand the matter.

"Now I'll tell you what's a fact," said Perk. "Suppose you do smell smoke ; what of it?"

"Why thar's a fire around here somewhere," answered the trapper; " an' whar thar's a fire thar must have been somebody to set it agoin'."

The boys understood it now, and exhibited no little surprise. They snuffed the air repeatedly, but their senses were not as keen as those of the trappers, and they could detect no smell of smoke. But Dick and old Bob could, and they followed it up with all the sagacity of a brace of hounds. They skirted the hills for a quarter of a mile or more, breasting the fierce wind which almost took their breath away, and then Dick suddenly reined his horse into the willows. He kept straight ahead, turning neither to the right nor left, and presently brought his companions within sight of the fire.

The boys were greatly disappointed. They had confidently expected to find Archie and his friends there, but they saw no one except a solitary stranger, who was doubled up over a small bed of coals, rubbing his palms together and shaking violently in every limb. His hands and face were blue with cold. He glanced up as they approached, and then looked down into the fire again.

"Hallo, stranger!" cried Dick. "Whar mought you be a travellin' to?"

"I'm lost," was the faint reply, "an' starvin' an' freezin'."

"Sho!" exclaimed the trapper; "freezin' with a fire in front of you an' all this timber around you!"

"Boys," said Uncle Dick, "unpack the provisions, a couple of you, and the rest of us cut some wood.   This poor fellow is so nearly benumbed that he can't keep his fire going."

A few minutes' work made a great change in the appearance of the stranger's camp.   Three or four small trees had been cut down for the horses to browse upon; the fire was roaring cheerfully; a coffee-pot and several slices of bacon were spattering on the coals; and the bushes and saplings had been cleared away for a space of twenty feet or more, and piled on one side of the camp to protect it from the fury of the wind.   The kind-hearted and thoughtful George, noticing that the stranger's well-worn clothing was but a poor protection against the wintry blasts, had thrown a pair of heavy blankets over his shoulders; but he was so cold that he hugged the fire long after all the rest had begun to back away from it.   The boys were eager to hear how he came there, but old Bob restrained their impatience.   " A man that's hungry an' half froze can't talk," said he.   " Wait till he gets warmed up with a pot or two of hot coffee, an' stows away a few pounds of them bacon an' crackers, an' his tongue will run lively enough, I tell you."

The old trapper was mistaken for once, however. The stranger emptied his cup as fast as it was filled for him, and disposed of three men's share of the bacon and biscuits, but they seemed to have no effect on his tongue. He was as dumb as a wooden man, and seemed uneasy in the presence of those who had fed and warmed him.

At length Uncle Dick began questioning him, telling him also that if he would let them know where he wanted to go the trappers would put him on his course; and furthermore, they would give him provisions enough to last him until he reached his destination. He finally succeeded in getting the stranger started on his story, which he told in such a way that none of his auditors believed a word of it. He said he had belonged to a wagon-train which had been attacked by the Indians. The most of the emigrants had been massacred, all the stock driven off and he had barely escaped with

his life.   It happened a week ago,* and he had had
nothing to eat since.

Uncle Dick and his party heard him through,
and then settled back and looked their disbelief.
If there had been any Indian depredations during
the week that had just passed, Colonel Gaylord
would not have been ignorant of the fact, and they
would have been certain to have heard of it through
him.   The impression at once became general that
the man had been doing something that would not
bear investigation, else why had he trumped up
such a story?   They made no remark, however,
and it is probable that the stranger would have been
permitted to go his way without any further questioning or offers of assistance from them, had it not
been for one little circumstance.   There was a wit-
ness against him which he had not thought of, and
Frank was the one who discovered it.   The latter,
who was sitting on the opposite side of the fire with
his hands clasping his knees, suddenly straightened
up and looked closely at something lying on the
ground by the stranger's side.   Presently he arose

and walking over to him, laid hold of the object, which was concealed from the view of the others by the blankets that George Le Dell had thrown over the man's shoulders. As he made an effort to lift it, the stranger seized it and held it fast. The expression on Frank's face brought the Club to their feet in a twinkling.

"Let go," said Frank, earnestly. "I want to see what you've got here."

"It's mine," said the stranger.

"Well, I must see it and know how you came by it. Let go."

The man still held fast to the object, whatever it was, and Frank, seizing it with both hands wrenched it out of his grasp, jerking off the blankets at the same time, and bringing to light a Maynard rifle— the mate to his own. It was so much like it, in fact, that when the rifles were first purchased by the cousins, they could never tell them apart until they had had their names engraved on them. Frank was so well acquainted with the weapon that he would have known it had he seen it in Asia. He turned it up, and there was Archie's name on the butt-plate. He read the name aloud, and the boys flocked about him with exclamations of wonder, each one taking the rifle into his own hands and giving it a good looking over. It was so unexpected, this finding of Archie's property in the possession of a stranger, that they wanted the evidence of their own eyes before they could believe it.

"Now I'll just tell you what's a fact," said Perk, who was the first to speak, "you've been up to something. Where did you get it?"

"Hand out the cartridges," said Frank, finding that there was an empty shell in the chamber of the rifle.

"What's that thar stickin' out thar?" exclaimed old Bob, suddenly.

Bab pushed away the stranger's leg and snatched up a belt containing two revolvers. They were Eugene's, and every one about the fire recognised them.

"You've been up to something, I tell you," said Perk.

"Hand out the cartridges," repeated Frank.

"I hain't got none," replied Simon Cool, for it was he. "I didn't have but one load for the rifle, and I tried to get something to eat with that."

"When did you last see the boys who own these things?" asked Uncle Dick.

"Two days ago."

"How many of them were they, and were they all right?"

Simon replied that there were three of them, and that the last time he saw them they were safe and sound, and in no danger of suffering from cold or hunger; and then, in obedience to Uncle Dick's command, went on to tell his story—the true story this time—to which his auditors listened with much more attention than they had given when he related his first one. He told everything just as we have told it, and when his story was ended, Dick Lewis declared that they had rested long enough, and ordered an immediate start.

The sorrow which Simon Cool pretended to feel for the wrong he had done, did not secure his release, as he had hoped it would. Uncle Dick did not know how much faith to put in him. They might not find the boys where Simon said he had left them; or if they did find them, they might not be all right after all. Then, too, they might have more to tell than Simon had seen fit to disclose; and taking all these things into consideration, Uncle Dick decided that the man should be detained until they had opportunity to satisfy themselves of the truth of his statements.

Frank's horse, being the largest and strongest animal in the party, was given over to Dick Lewis, who took Simon up behind him and carried him during the rest of the journey. So impatient were they all to find the missing boys, that their halts were few and far between, and they made such good headway, in spite of the snow-drifts, that they reached the mouth of the gully on the afternoon of the second day after the finding of Simon Cool. The gully was filled with snow, and as it had not been recently disturbed, they knew that the boys were still finding shelter under the cliffs.

While Dick and Bob were breaking a road for the horses, the former, whose eyes were everywhere, called Frank's attention to something. It was a smooth, bare spot on a beech tree, from which the bark had been cleared by a knife or hatchet. Frank became excited at once. He floundered through a deep drift, brushed the snow off the tree, and calling the attention of his companions, read aloud the following, which had been written with a lead-pencil:

"Nov. 12th.—All well and hearty, but don't like being weather-bound. If we must be snowed up again, should rather have it done in summer. Take the first right-hand gully, then the *next* right-hand one, and you will find us before you have gone a quarter of a mile."

"Well, the boys are in good heart," said Uncle Dick, and the long breath that came up from his broad chest showed the relief he felt.

"I knowed we'd find them keerless fellers all right," said Dick Lewis.

"And here's something else that I can't quite

make out," said Frank, still studying the writing on the tree. "Archie always writes a horrible hand when he's in a hurry."

"Perhaps his fingers were cold," said Walter.

"It is dated November 16," continued Frank.

"That was yesterday," said Uncle Dick, with some uneasiness. "No bad news, I hope. Try and make it out if you can."

Frank lightly brushed off the snow, taking care not to erase the pencil-marks, and then slowly read, spelling out each word, a sentence that created as great a commotion as a thunderbolt would have done, had it suddenly fallen into the midst of the party:

"We have found Chase, and he is well."

"*What!*" cried Uncle Dick.

"That's what I make it," said Frank, breaking away from the tree to make room for Perk and the rest of the boys, who came plunging through the drift. "I shouldn't wonder if your missing friend had turned up at last."

"WE HAVE FOUND CHASE."

" Yes, sir, he has !" exclaimed Bob, after he had closely examined the writing ; " hasn't he, Perk ?"

Perk took a look, then Walter and George, and each declared that Frank's rendering of the obscure sentence was the correct one. The boys were so surprised and delighted that they could scarcely speak.

" Well ! well ! I never will be surprised at anything again," said Uncle Dick. " There are some people away off in Louisiana who would give something to know what we know now. Push ahead, Lewis. You can't go any too fast for us."

" Look a yer," said Simon Cool, suddenly. " Seein' you've found your friends, mightn't you as well turn me loose ?"

" Why, man, you would freeze or starve," said Bob.

" I kin take keer of myself," replied Simon, who, it was plain, would much rather have taken his chances on the prairie than face those whom he had wronged.

" We have another story to listen to before we

take leave of you," said Uncle Dick.   " Climb up, boys, and we'll be off."

The whole party were in their saddles in two minutes more, and riding down the gully as fast as the deep snow-drifts would permit.

CHAPTER XIII.

THE STOWAWAY.

TURN we now to follow, briefly, the fortunes of Henry Chase, who had for so many months been an object of solicitude to the old members of the Sportsman's Club, and the rest of his friends living in Louisiana.

It will be remembered that when this young gentleman and his crony, Wilson, were first introduced to the reader, they were not on the best of terms with Walter and his party. They belonged to Bayard Bell's boat-club, made common cause with him in everything, and on one occasion came to an open rupture with the crew of the Zephyr, and might have got into a fight with them, had it not been for the timely arrival of Mr. Gaylord and Uncle Dick. This happened on the day of the panther-hunt, which

13

was the beginning of the adventures we have attempted to describe in the *Sportsman's Club Series*.

Shortly after that, on the very same day in fact, some things came to light which made a wonderful change in the feelings of these two boys. They found that the unreasonable enmity which Bayard cherished toward the members of the Sportsman's Club was likely to get him, and all connected with him, into serious trouble; so they abruptly deserted him, and made an attempt to warn Walter Gaylord of the plans that were being laid against him. They failed in their efforts, however, and got themselves into a scrape; and there is no telling what might have become of Chase, had not the Sportsman's Club fortunately discovered him hidden away under a pile of leaves on Lost Island, where the smugglers had left him, and rendered him assistance. Wilson was Chase's steadfast friend ; and to show their gratitude to the Club, he and Chase joined their vessel, the Banner, and accompanied them to Cuba, to assist in rescuing Fred Craven, who was a prisoner on board the Stella, of which Mr. Bell was the owner.

They bore an important part in that memorable expedition, and when left in charge of the vessel by Walter, were decoyed away by a note written by Mr. Bell's directions, and sent out into the country, to the house of one Don Casper Nevis, the agent whose business it was to receive the arms and ammunition that were smuggled into the island for the use of the Cuban rebels. While on the way to the Don's house they were seen, suspected and watched by a squad of government patrols, who made an attempt to arrest them; but they were saved by their host, who concealed them in a wine-cellar until dark, and then brought them out, and made ready to furnish them with horses to take them back to Port Platte.

Now, it happened that the Don had all the while been under a wrong impression in regard to the character of the two boys who were his guests. A note, which was brought to him by the negro who had acted as a guide to Chase and Wilson, and which was written by Captain Conway, the master of Mr. Bell's smuggling schooner, led the Don to

believe that the boys belonged to the Stella, and
that they had been sent out there to make arrange-
ments in regard to the landing of her contraband
cargo. Chase tried to correct this wrong impression, and to explain to the Don how they came to
be in Cuba, and the consequence was that he got
himself and Wilson into a worse predicament than
they had ever been in before. The Don was highly
enraged, and refused to believe a word of their
story. He accused them of being Spanish spies,
who had been sent out to his house on purpose to
give the patrols some excuse for arresting him,
declared that he would take them forthwith before
Captain Conway, and if he could not vouch for
them, they might make up their minds that some
terrible punishment would be visited upon them.
The Don then went after the horses, and Chase and
Wilson were left in charge of his overseer, who had
orders to shoot them down if they attempted to
escape.

The boys both realized that they were in a very
unenviable situation, and the question was how to

get out of it. Captain Conway would not vouch for them, that was certain. He would declare that he had never seen them before, and that would be all that was needed to confirm the Don's suspicions. Then what would become of them? Wilson was disposed to trust to luck, but Chase had more confidence in his legs. He resolved to run away, leaving Walter and the rest to look out for themselves, and make all haste to get out of Cuba. He would ship on the first vessel he could find, no matter if she took him to South America. He waited anxiously for an opportunity to slip away from the overseer, and it was quickly presented to him.

Tomlinson and the rest of the deserters from the revenue cutter, who had stolen a passage to Cuba in the Banner, appeared on the scene about this time, the object of their visit to the plantation being to procure the provisions necessary to serve them during their voyage to Havana, where they expected to join a Cuban privateer. While these worthies were forcing an entrance into the storehouse, and Wilson and the overseer were watching them, Chase slipped away in the darkness. Had he waited two minutes longer, he might have escaped in company with his friend. Wilson also eluded the vigilance of the overseer, went on board the Banner which was anchored in the bay, and with her returned to the States in time to take part in the Christmas festivities at the hospitable Gaylord mansion; but Chase became a wanderer upon the face of the earth, and was not even heard of for nearly a year.

Chase moved very slowly and cautiously until he was out of sight of the overseer, and then he ran as he had never run before. His first object was to put a safe distance between himself and the store-house; and when that had been done, he made a wide circuit to avoid the dwelling and the Spanish troopers who were keeping guard over it, and at last reached the road which led to the village of Port Platte. Then he slackened his pace to a rapid walk and began to breathe easier. His escape had been easily accomplished, and now he had only to go to the town and find some ship that was to sail at once;

the sooner the better, if he were but allowed to get fairly over the side. If she were bound for the States, well and good; but rather than remain longer in Cuba he would ship on a vessel bound for Greenland. Life in the forecastle or among the icebergs was much to be preferred to a longer sojourn in such a country as this, where every man suspected his neighbor, and Spanish troopers were always ready to arrest people for the most-trivial causes and shoot them down without ceremony. Chase wished now that he had not read the papers quite so attentively. Every act of cruelty which he had seen recorded came to his mind with startling distinctness, and stayed there too, in spite of all his efforts to banish it. He began to miss his friend Wilson already. The latter had been cheerful and hopeful in spite of all their misfortunes, and his example and words of encouragement had done much to keep up Chase's drooping spirits. He would have given something now to have had anybody for companion, for it was anything but pleasant to be friendless and alone in that strange country. Every

road and by-way was guarded by patrols, and what
if he should happen to fall into the hands of some
of them?   He could only account for his presence
in Cuba by telling a very improbable story, and if
the patrols should refuse to believe it, and he could
not find Walter and the rest to prove what he said,
he might perhaps be detained and punished as a spy.

"I wish I had never seen or heard of the Sportsman's Club," said Chase, for the twentieth time.
"They've got themselves and me into a pretty
scrape, and there is no one to be benefited by it.
I'd give something to know what has become of the
rest of the fellows.   I'll warrant that I'll see home
before they will."

The moon began to struggle through the clouds
now—it was just about this time that Wilson
was running his race with Pierre for the yawl—and
this was a point in Chase's favor, for it enabled him
to see every object in the road in advance of him.
He kept a bright lookout for the dreaded patrols,
and was ready to take to the bushes at the first sight
of a horseman; but the guards, which had been as

plenty as blackberries during the day-time, were not to be seen, and Chase accomplished his ten-mile walk without meeting anybody. The plantation houses along the road were as dark and silent as if they had been deserted, and even the dogs, which had greeted him and Wilson so vociferously when they passed that way in the day-time, were neither seen nor heard.

The road led Chase straight to the wide, arched gateway which opened upon the wharf near the place where the Banner was moored when he last saw her. The Spanish brig was still there, and Chase hurriedly clambered over her rail and ran to the opposite side. He did not expect to find Walter's vessel there, and consequently he was neither surprised nor disappointed when he found that her berth was empty. The gallant little Banner, under the charge of her lawful captain, who had recovered her in a most unexpected manner, was at that moment running out of the bay at the rear of the Don's plantation, having safely passed the iron-clad frigate that had been sent in pursuit of her.

"Aha!" said Chase, in a triumphant tone, "I knew I wasn't quite so foolish as some people gave me credit for. Won't Wilson be in a nice fix when he comes here with the Don? He expects to find the Banner here, and is relying upon Walter and the rest to prove who he is and how he came here; but he'll not find them, and I knew he wouldn't. I wouldn't be in his boots for anything. Why didn't he run away when I did?"

Chase, congratulating himself on having shown no small degree of shrewdness and generalship in the way he had managed matters during the last few hours, turned to go back to the wharf. One of the brig's crew who recognised him, and who knew by his actions that he was looking for the Banner, addressed a few words to him, waving his arm toward the Gulf and saying "boom! boom!" a great many times. He was trying to explain to the boy that the Banner had gone out, and that she had been fired at by the guns of the Fort; but Chase could not understand a word he said, and believing that the sailor was making game of him, he sprang over the brig's side and hurried away.

His first care was to satisfy himself that the Stella still occupied her old berth, and that none of her company were roaming about the wharf. Chase had learned to stand in wholesome fear of Mr. Bell and his gang of smugglers, and he did not care to meet any of them again if he could help it. But Mr. Bell was no longer in a situation to do him any injury, if he had only known it. If he had approached close enough to the Stella he must have gained some idea of the state of affairs, for he would have seen the soldiers on her deck. He *did* see a number of men walking about, but he was too far away to see their uniforms, and believing that the moving figures were members of her crew on watch, he hurried away as fast as his legs could carry him, to find a vessel that was about to sail.

"And what if I shouldn't happen to find one?" Chase almost gasped, a new and most unwelcome thought suddenly forcing itself upon him. "In a little out-of-the-way port like this, vessels can't be coming and going at all hours of the day and night, and if I can't get off, where shall I sleep, and where shall I go in the morning to get something to eat?"

Chase was called upon more than once to decide such questions as these before he saw home and friends again. Indeed, there were a few weeks of his life during which the finding of food to sustain life, and a shelter of some kind to protect him while he slept, about which he had never before bothered his head, were matters that occupied every one of his waking hours. But on this occasion fortune seemed to favor him. A few steps from the Spanish brig lay a ship which Chase had noticed during the day. It was then being loaded, and the anxiety manifested by the officers to get the freight aboard as rapidly as possible, indicated that she was about to leave port. Toward this vessel Chase bent his steps, and he was overjoyed to find that the loading was all done, and that preparations were being made to take her to sea. Some of the lines were already cast off, and a couple of men in a yawl were making an effort to tow her bow out from the wharf. Chase had arrived just in time. He made all haste to get on board, and while he was looking about for the captain, to whom he wished to make known his desires, he was accosted by a bustling little man in a red shirt and wide trowsers, who proved to be the second mate of the vessel.

"Now, then, what do you want here?" exclaimed that gentleman. "Off you go. We're going to sea at once."

"I am glad to hear it," replied Chase. "I want to ship."

"Too late," said the mate. "Got a full crew already. Lay aft, a couple of you," he added, as a hoarse voice shouted out some orders from the quarter-deck. "If you are not ashore in half a minute, my lad, you'll have to go with us."

The mate hurried away to attend to his duties, and Chase, who would have tried to gain his ear a moment longer, was left to himself.

"Where are you bound?" he asked of a man who at that moment ran past him—"for the States?"

The sailor, whose actions indicated that he had no

time to waste in answering foolish questions, made
a motion with his head, the significance of which
was very doubtful; but Chase took it for a reply in
the affirmative, and his mind was made up on the
instant.   Here was the opportunity he had been
longing for, and the only thing that prevented him
from taking advantage of it, was the fact that the
crew was full.   But that made no difference to
Chase.   His circumstances were desperate, and in
his opinion desperate measures were required.   Instead of going ashore, as he had been ordered to do,
he looked about the deck, and having made sure
that all the crew, from the captain down, were too
busy to pay any attention to himself, he suddenly
crouched down beside one of the boats that had been
stowed in the waist, and crawled under it out of
sight.

"There!" panted Chase, whose heart beat violently with excitement and suspense; "if I can only
stay here five minutes without being discovered, I
shall be all right.   They'll not stop to put me ashore
after they once get fairly started.   I don't know

what the captain will say to me when he finds me here, and I don't care, so long as he gives me plenty to eat and takes me to my own country. It is enough for me to know that I am leaving Cuba behind every minute."

Chase was securely hidden under the boat, and not one of the crew, who were constantly passing his hiding-place, suspected his presence. The work of hoisting the sails was completed at last, and finally the vessel began to rise and fall with a slow regular motion, telling the stowaway that she had left the sheltered waters of the harbor, and was fairly afloat on the Gulf.

And now came a task which Chase would have been glad to postpone indefinitely if he could. He must come out and show himself to the captain.

CHAPTER XIV.

A LONG WAY HOME.

CHASE remained in his concealment for a long time, trying to make up some plausible story to tell the captain in reply to the rigid cross-examination which he knew he would have to undergo when he first appeared before that gentleman. The captain would, of course, want to know how he came to be in Cuba, and why he was in so great a hurry to leave it, and Chase did not expect him to believe the story he had to tell. The captain of the revenue cutter had refused to believe it when Walter told it to him; Don Casper had pronounced it false; and it was reasonable to suppose that the master of the ship would do the same. But it was all true, no matter whether people thought so or not; and Chase finally making up his mind that truth would hold its own with falsehood any day,

abandoned the idea of making up a story, and resolved to tell just what had occurred, leaving the
captain to do as he pleased about believing it.   He
would do it at once, too.   The sooner it was over
and he knew what was to be done with him, the
better he would feel.

With this thought in his mind Chase arose quickly
from his concealment, bumping his head against the
side of the boat as he did so, and when he got upon
his feet, found himself standing face to face with
the second mate, who started back and looked at
him, being too surprised to speak.   Believing that
when the officer recovered himself the first words
he uttered would be a volley of oaths, Chase
hastened to account for his presence by saying:

"You told me that if I didn't go ashore I would
have to sail with you, and I thought, from the way
you said it, that you wouldn't be very angry if I
should go with you.   I want to work my passage
home."

" Well, here's a go," said the officer, looking all
14

around the vessel and then fastening his eyes on Chase again.

"I shan't be any expense to you," continued the boy, "for I am able to earn the food I eat. I don't know anything about square-rigged vessels, but I know something about schooner-rigged yachts, and I can stand my trick at the wheel with almost anybody."

While Chase was talking the mate had time to collect himself. He walked to the side of the vessel, threw out his quid of tobacco, and then came back. His words were not very reassuring, but the tone in which they were uttered delighted Chase, for it satisfied him that if all the officers of the ship were like this one, he had nothing to fear.

"I suppose I ought to throw you overboard," said the mate. "You ran away from home to be a sailor, did you? And you're sick of your bargain too, are you? It serves you just right," he added, with a glance at the boy's white hands and broad-cloth suit, the latter beginning to show the effects of the hard treatment it had received during the last few days. "You'll stay at home with your mother when you get there again, won't you?"

"I didn't run away," said Chase, as soon as he saw a chance to speak. "I have a good home, and I am anxious to get back to it."

"Ah! yes," said the mate, with a nod that spoke volumes. "Home looks very comfortable and pleasant after one has been away from it a while, don't it? Well, the old man's turned in, and you can't see him till to-morrow. I don't know what to do with you, so you had better go below, and if you can find an empty bunk, turn in and go to sleep."

"Thank you," said Chase, gratefully. "I shall be very glad to do it."

The boy made his way to the forecastle, feeling as if a heavy burden had been removed from his shoulders. Like most people who get their ideas of men and things solely from books, he had formed some very erroneous opinions. He had believed that all sailors, and especially all mates, were brutes, who asked no better amusement than swearing at somebody or knocking him down with a handspike. But here was a mate who was a very different sort of person, and he was glad indeed that he had fallen in with him.

The forecastle—a dark, badly-ventilated apartment in the forward part of the vessel, smelling of tar and bilge-water, and dimly lighted by a smoky lantern—was not quite as inviting a place to sleep as his airy room at home, or even the cosy, nicely-furnished cabin of the Banner; but it was better than no shelter at all, and Chase thought he could stand it during the five or six days that would probably elapse before he reached New Orleans. Several of the bunks were occupied by the men belonging to the watch below, and the beds that were made up in the others showed that they belonged to the sailors who were on deck. There were two empty ones, however, in the lowest tier and in the farthest corner of the forecastle, and of one of these Chase took possession, blessing his lucky stars that at last he had an opportunity to rest his tired limbs. The pine boards that composed the bottom of the bunk were rather hard, but he was among his own countrymen, and Mr. Bell and Cuba were being left farther behind every moment. Of course he had no bedding, that being something that every sailor is expected to furnish for himself. He had his hat for a pillow, and while he was arranging it under his head, and trying to find a board in the bottom of the bunk soft enough to sleep upon, he became aware that a sailor in the opposite berth was greatly interested in his movements. Indeed, when he came to look about him, he found that the eyes of all the men in the forecastle were directed toward his bunk.

"Well, mates," said Chase, in an off-hand, easy manner, which he thought becoming to a sailor, "is this the first time you ever saw a stowaway?"

"That's how you came aboard, is it?" said one of the men. "I thought I hadn't seen you before."

"Yes, I have stolen my passage," replied Chase. "I wanted to ship, but they told me they had all the men they needed. I was bound to leave Cuba, however, so I hid under the long boat till the ship was well out to sea.   The mate sent me down here till the captain gets ready to see me."

Chase expected to be the butt of a good many jokes and smart remarks from the sailors, so when they began upon him he was prepared to submit. But, after all, they had nothing very aggravating to say, and finding that he received their pleasantries very good-naturedly, they finally desisted and left him to sleep in peace—all except the sailor in the opposite bunk, who seemed to have a larger share of curiosity than his companions, and showed a desire to know something of the boy's history. He smiled and nodded his head, just as the mate had done, while he listened to Chase's account of his recent adventures, and when the boy finished his story, asked him where he lived.

"In Bellville, Louisiana," replied Chase.

"Well, seems to me you're taking a long way to get home," said the sailor, as he pulled the blankets over his shoulders and turned his face to the bulkhead preparatory to going to sleep.

"How is that? One of the crew told me that the ship is bound for the States."

"So she is; but she is going by the way of the Horn and Good Hope."

"Great goodness! Around the world!" exclaimed Chase, as soon as he could speak.

The sailor replied that that was what some people called a voyage of that kind, and then settled himself between the blankets, while Chase sat bolt upright in his bunk, staring blankly about him.

"Around the world!" he kept saying to himself, as if he could not quite understand the words. He had not bargained for any such extended tour as that, and he was not prepared for it. Could he live for long months, and perhaps years, without any bedding to sleep on, and no clothes except those he then wore? And what would the folks at home think had become of him? Poor Chase was almost overwhelmed at the thought of so long a separation from his friends, and appalled by the dangers, both real and imaginary, which he saw looming up before him; and he wished now, when it was too late, that

he had not been in so great a hurry to get out of
Cuba. He would willingly have gone back to the
Don's wine-cellar—he was almost willing to say that
he would rather be a prisoner in the hands of the
Spaniards than be in his present situation. He
never closed his eyes in sleep. All the night long he
rolled about in his bunk, thinking over his troubles ;
and he was glad when the morning dawned, and the
mate came into the forecastle to tell him that the
captain wanted to see him on the quarter-deck.

Almost too weak and dispirited to move, Chase
managed to follow the officer up the ladder, and in
a few seconds more he was standing, hat in hand,
before the master of the vessel—a gray-headed old
gentleman, who reminded Chase of Uncle Dick
Gaylord. He proved to be like Uncle Dick, too, in
more respects than one, which was a fortunate thing
for the stowaway. He was evidently prepared to
say something severe, for his forehead wore a
threatening scowl ; but when his eyes rested on the
crying youth before him, his face softened at once.

"Well, my lad," said he, "don't you know that you have no business here?"

"Yes, sir," replied Chase.

"What have you to say for yourself?"

The boy had a good deal to say for himself, and it took him some time to say it, although he related his story with all haste, touching only on such portions of it as he thought would interest the captain. The latter listened patiently, but with evident surprise, and when Chase ceased speaking, said:

"I saw the yacht you describe, and noticed that there was a good deal going on aboard of her. Were you the boy who jumped overboard?"

"No, sir," replied Chase, wondering what the captain meant.

"Were you on her when she was under the fire of the fort?"

The boy began to open his eyes now. These questions made it plain to him that he and Wilson were not the only ones who had seen excitement and been in perilous situations during the afternoon. The rest of the yacht's company had come in for a share, but of course Chase knew nothing about it, for he was ten miles away in the country, and part of the time locked up in the Don's wine-cellar.

"As you are here and I can't well put you ashore, I shall do the best I can by you," said the captain. "Of course you have no outfit?"

"Nothing except the clothes I stand in," replied Chase.

"Then you had better sign articles at boy's wages, and after that you can go to the slop-chest."

"Very well, sir," replied Chase, who did not quite catch the captain's meaning. "I suppose I can do no better."

"I will discharge you at San Francisco, which will be the first port in America at which we shall touch."

So saying the captain walked down into his cabin, followed by Chase. The boy signed his name to the shipping articles, and was then turned over to the steward, who was told to conduct him to the slop-chest and give him what he wanted.

"I was in hopes I should be allowed to mess with

the men," said Chase, as the steward led him away. "I am one of the crew now, and I don't think I ought to be fed on slops."

The steward stared at him a moment, and then broke out into a hearty fit of laughter.

"Did you ever see a ship before?" he asked.

"O, yes," replied Chase. "I live in a seaport town."

"Well, did you never hear that greenhorns always mess in the crow's-nest, and that their skouse and dough-boy are cooked in tar and bilge-water?"

"No, I never did."

"Well, it is a fact, as you will find. It hardens their muscles and makes them water-proof."

Chase simply smiled his disbelief, and followed the steward below, where the ship's supplies were kept. Then he found that the slop-chest was not a chest after all. It was the ship's variety store—a little locker in which were stowed away an abundance of mattresses, blankets, trowsers, shirts, pea-jackets, needles, thread, tobacco and other articles of necessity and luxury which go to make up a sailor's kit.

"O, things are not so bad after all," thought Chase, as he gazed at the well-filled shelves. "They might be a great deal worse. I shall not freeze while going around the Horn, and neither shall I starve; and when I am once safe ashore at San Francisco, it will not be much of a task to work my way home across the plains. I shall see something of life and of the world, too. I believe I'd rather be here than in the Don's wine-cellar."

The steward assisted him in making his selections, charging each article to his account at rather higher prices than he would have had to pay ashore, and when he had got all he wanted he carried them to the forecastle and stowed them away in his bunk. After that he was ordered into the cabin to assist the steward, and in two days more was fairly settled in his new position, and knew how to scour knives and bang dishes as well as the other cabin-boy.

Before many days had passed over his head,

Chase was effectually cured of some very foolish notions, just as many another deluded boy has been cured. It may be all very well for those who go to sea as passengers to write in glowing terms of the ease and romance of a sailor's life, but one who is before the mast, and has the work to do, must of necessity look at it in a different light. Chase found it one of drudgery and toil. There was always something to do, for shipmasters believe that men cannot be kept in a proper state of discipline unless they are constantly busy. Chase had his duties on deck to perform as well as his work in the cabin; for when sail was made or shortened, all hands and the cook were called upon to assist. Then, too, the position he occupied was menial—he was emphatically a servant of servants, as every greenhorn is at sea. The men in the forecastle called upon him to wait on them, and even the other cabin-boy, who, although a year younger than himself, had made one voyage in the ship, exercised authority over him, and shifted upon his shoulders the responsibility of keeping the captain's boots well blacked. He had to wait at table, and stand behind the captain's chair while that gentleman was eating his meals, just as one of his own father's negro servants had done during the days of slavery.

All this was extremely galling to Chase, who was a high-spirited, aristocratic young fellow; but he had too much good sense to make his situation worse by rebelling. He performed his duties carefully and patiently, acting on a hint his sensible father had once given him, and which he constantly bore in mind. "Henry," said Mr. Chase, on one occasion, "if it is your fortune in life to be a bottle-cleaner, see to it that you make the bottles *shine*."

Chase made the plates and the knives and forks shine, but he chafed inwardly while he was doing it, and told himself over and over again that he could not think of any combination of circumstances that would ever induce him, of his own free will, to go to sea as a foremast hand or a cabin-boy.

With some of his surroundings Chase was agreeably surprised. While he was on board the Petrel—

that was the name of the ship—he did not hear an oath uttered by either officers or men, or see a blow struck. The captain was a man who did not permit such things. In this respect Chase's experience was very different from that of another of his friends, whose adventures in the forecastle we have yet to relate.

During the voyage scarcely an incident happened that was worthy of notice. The first port in which the Petrel dropped her anchor was Callao, where she remained nearly a month. The next was Honolulu, in the Sandwich Islands. Here another long and, to Chase, extremely vexatious delay occurred; but the cargo was discharged at last, a new one taken aboard, and the Petrel spread her wings for California. Propelled by favoring breezes she made a quick run, and finally the Golden Gate was passed, and the anchor dropped in the harbor of San Francisco. One of the boats was called away to take the captain ashore, and just as it was ready to start, Chase was summoned into the cabin and presented with his discharge, and a five-dollar bill. The money was a present from the captain, and was something he did not expect. He had kept a strict run of his accounts, and knew that the articles he had drawn from the slop-chest footed up a dollar or two more than his wages.

With a light heart Chase gathered up his clothes and blankets, leaving his mattress, which was too bulky to go in his bundle, as a gift to one of the sailors, and taking his seat in the captain's boat was soon landed on the wharf. He was alone in a strange city, with scarcely more than money enough in his pocket to take him fairly out of its limits, and the whole world was before him.

CHAPTER XV.

A CHEAP BOARDING-HOUSE.

CHASE had waited and longed for the hour of his liberation, and now that it had arrived, he did not enjoy it as he had thought he would. He looked at the ship which had been his home for so many long months, then at the captain, who had won his heart by the kindness and consideration with which he had always treated him, and had half a mind to turn back and ask to be received again as one of the crew. But there was that long voyage that the Petrel had yet to make, and Chase had grown heartily weary of the blue water and hard ship's fare. The vessel was going, in the first place, back to the Sandwich Islands, then to China, and home by the way of the Cape of Good Hope; and no one on board of her knew just how long it

15

would take to make the voyage.   Before it was half
over, Chase hoped to be among friends once more.

With a long-drawn sigh the boy hurried away,
and so very much engrossed was he with his thoughts
that he missed seeing something that would have
astonished him beyond measure, and might have
been the means of saving him from many hardships
and privations that he afterward suffered.   During
the time he had been on board the Petrel, Uncle
Dick Gaylord's schooner had been launched, and
had made her voyage around the Horn to San
Francisco.   She was now lying at her anchorage in
the harbor, and she attracted Chase's attention,
just as she attracted the notice of everybody, sailor
or landsman, who passed that way.   He did not
look at her, however, until after he had passed her
stern, on which were painted her name and the name
of the port to which she belonged—"Stranger:
Bellville."

How Chase's heart would have throbbed could he
have seen those two words!   He knew nothing of
the extended tour his friends had undertaken, for

the Club themselves had not known of it, until that memorable Christmas morning when Uncle Dick revealed to them the secret to which he had so often alluded. Chase never dreamed that that little vessel had brought Walter and the rest to that part of the world, and that she was waiting there until they should return from their trip over the mountains. The man in blue, who was leaning over her rail, looking at him as he passed, could have told him all about it, if Chase had known enough to ask him; but the boy only just glanced at him, ran his eye over the schooner, said to himself that she was a beautiful little craft, and undoubtedly a "trotter," and then throwing his bundle down beside a warehouse, seated himself on it to think over his situation, and decide upon his future movements; for, as yet, he had not been able to make up his mind what he ought to do, although he had been constantly turning the matter over in his mind ever since he learned that he was to be discharged at San Francisco. He must make up his mind to something before he wrote to his father, so that he could tell him just what he intended to do, and Mr. Chase might know where to send assistance or meet him in case of necessity. But the longer he pondered the matter, the more undecided he became; and he finally resolved to begin the letter, hoping that before it was completed something would suggest itself to him.

Having come to this determination, Chase shouldered his bundle and hurried away again. He went up one street and down another, and finally, as he was passing along, glanced through an open door into what proved to be the reading-room of a hotel. There were several gentlemen in the room, some absorbed in their papers, others engaged in writing, and the long table was abundantly supplied with pens, ink and note-paper. Here was as good a place as he could find, Chase thought; so he entered without ceremony, deposited his bundle in one corner, and drew a chair up to the table. His entrance attracted the attention of several gentlemen, who looked at him in surprise, and one of them, after giving him a cold, impudent stare, got up and moved farther away from him.

"Suit yourself, my dear fellow," thought Chase. "Your room is as good as your company. I wonder if strangers are so unwelcome in this country that you feel called upon to insult every one you meet!"

He drew a sheet of paper toward him, picked up a pen and was about to dip it in the ink, when a dapper little clerk, with his hair parted in the middle, came up and slapped him on the shoulder.

"There is a sailor's boarding-house around the corner, two streets below here," said he, indicating the direction with the little finger of his left hand, which bore a large seal-ring.

"Is there?" said Chase. "Well, I am not looking for a sailor's boarding-house just now. I simply wish to write a letter."

"But you can't do it here," said the clerk, taking the pen from the boy's fingers. "None but gentlemen stop here. This is a first-class hotel."

"O, it is, is it?" exclaimed Chase, rising and picking up his bundle. "Then I should think the proprietors would employ first-class people for their servants."

Almost too angry to speak plainly, Chase made the best of his way to the street. This little incident reminded him of something of which he had always been aware, but which he had never expected to have brought home to him in this way, that distinctions exist on shore as well as on ship-board. The clothing he wore was against him. That hotel was for gentlemen only; and as a sailor is not supposed to be a gentleman, he could not stop there even long enough to write a letter to his father.

" Perhaps it serves me just right. I have been too much in the habit of judging people by their clothes, but I will never do it again," thought Chase, who now saw how unjust were the conclusions that might be drawn by measuring men and boys by such a standard. " I wonder if that clerk would have any greater respect for me if he knew that my father could buy him and his hotel! By the way——"

Here Chase stopped and looked down at the

ground a moment in a brown study, and then turned and slowly retraced his steps. Might it not be a good plan, after all, he asked himself, to take the clerk's advice and go to the sailor's boarding-house? It would be sheer folly for him to attempt the journey across the plains without any money in his pocket, and the best thing he could do would be to procure a cheap boarding-place, and stay there until he could receive assistance from home. He would write for money at once, and while it was coming he could find something to do that would bring him enough to pay his board. This was the best idea that had yet suggested itself to him, and Chase resolved to act upon it.

"Around the corner, two streets below," he thought, recalling the clerk's words, and glancing in at the reading-room as he passed. "I'll make it my business to come back here in a few days— just as soon as I can get some shore-clothes—and I'll see if that fellow will raise any objections to me then."

Chase easily found the house of which he was in

search, for its location was pointed out by a weather-beaten sign, bearing a picture that might once have represented a frigate under full sail ; but he was not very well pleased with it after he found it.   It was not as neat as he expected to see it.   Like the sign over the sidewalk, it was dingy and weather-stained, and some of the frosted panes in the windows were broken out, their places being supplied by rough boards and thick brown wrapping-paper, which were tacked over the holes.   The house looked as though it had passed through a battle, as indeed it had, several of them ; and if Chase had been there the night before, he would have seen the police make a raid upon it in force.   While he stood undecided whether to enter or look further for lodgings, the door opened, and a rough-looking man in his shirt-sleeves appeared on the threshold.   He had seen Chase through the window.

"Why, Jack, how de do?" he exclaimed, seizing the boy's hand and giving it a cordial grip and shake.   "When did your ship arrive?   Step right into the house.   I was looking for you and you were looking for me, I know. All the boys know where to come to get plenty to eat and drink."

Chase was surprised at this greeting. The man acted and talked as if he had seen him before. Without saying a word he allowed himself to be led into the house, surrendered his bundle when the landlord offered to take it from his hand, and seated himself in a chair pointed out to him.

Before the man addressed him again, Chase had a few moments' leisure in which to take a rapid survey of his surroundings. He saw enough in that time to make him wish that he had never come in there. The room was dirty in the extreme; the walls and the ceiling, the former adorned with cheap prints representing engagements at sea, were of a dingy brown color—made so, no doubt, by tobacco-smoke; the floor was covered with sawdust and littered with cigar-stumps, and a man dressed in the garb of a sailor was nodding in one corner. One end of the room was occupied by a bar, behind which the landlord was stowing away the bundle Chase had given him. Having done this, he placed a glass on the counter and gave the boy a friendly wink, the meaning of which the latter plainly understood.

"No, *sir*," said he, emphatically.

"Temperance?" asked the man.

"The worst kind," replied Chase.

"Stick to it. You'll be a captain some day."

"I think not," returned the boy; "I have had enough of sailoring already, and I'll never put my foot on a ship again as one of the crew. I will carry a hod on shore first."

"Ah! ran away from home, did you?"

"No, I did not. I shipped aboard the Petrel in Cuba, supposing that she was bound for the States; but she took me to the Sandwich Islands and then brought me here. I want to go home by the easiest and quickest route I can find, and I shall start as soon as I receive money from my father."

"You ain't strapped, be you?"

"Not quite. I want to write a letter to my father at once," continued Chase. "I shall hear from him in ten days or two weeks, and, in the meantime, I want some cheap place to stay."

"Well, you're in it now. You couldn't find a better place in Fr'isco. How much be you going to ask your father for?"

"I suppose it will take considerable money to buy me some shore-clothes and pay my railroad, stage and steamboat fare all the way home," said Chase, rather surprised at the question—"two hundred dollars, perhaps."

"Every cent of it, and more," said the man, slapping his hand on the counter. "Travelling is high, I can tell you. Is the old man rich?"

"He's got some money," answered Chase, who wondered how the man could tell that it would take more than two hundred dollars to pay his fare home when he did not know where he lived.

"Then ask him for three hundred. You'll need it all, and you can stay here till it comes. I won't charge you a cent, either. But, I say——"

Here the man came out from behind the counter,

drew a chair up by Chase's side, and slapping him
on the knee, said, in a confidential tone:

"I say, you'd best leave the money you've got
in my hands, as a sort of security, you know. I'll
take care of it for you. There's some pretty rough
fellows comes around here sometimes, and they
wouldn't mind taking it away from you, if they
knew you had it. Eh?"

"How much do you charge a day for boarding
and lodging?"

"A dollar."

"If I pay you every day as long as I stay here,
won't that satisfy you?"

"No, it won't. You see, if there's any robbing
and stealing done, I shall be blamed for it, because
I'm sorter responsible for you while you are here."

"You needn't be. I can take care of myself.
Besides, I may conclude not to stay with you, you
know. I shall probably find some place I like better," said the boy, glancing about the room.

"O, you'll stay, I'll bet you on that," said the

landlord, with a laugh and a look that Chase did not like.

"I don't think you will compel me to stay against my will," said the boy, rising to his feet. "I have no desire to stop in a house frequented by men who do 'robbing and stealing.' I think I can find more agreeable quarters. At any rate, I will look around a little before I decide. I'll trouble you for my bundle."

"And I'll trouble you to sit down," said the man, pushing him back into his chair. "You needn't think you're going to go out on the street to carry tales to the police about my house."

"I have no intention of doing anything of the kind, for I don't know anything about your hotel, and I don't want to," said Chase, trying hard to keep up a bold front, although his heart sank within him.

The boy had been in the house scarcely ten min-utes, and he began to see that he had got himself into trouble by coming there. He was in one of those low sailor boarding-houses of which he had heard and read so much, kept by a man known as a "landshark," who, while he pretended to make a business of feeding and sheltering seafaring men, gained the principal part of his living by robbing them. Those who came into his house with full pockets, never took a cent out with them. Probably his cupidity had been excited by the mention of the large amount that Chase expected his father to send him immediately upon the receipt of his letter. If he could keep the boy there until the money arrived, Chase would never see a cent of it. He would retain it all himself, and wind up the business by shipping his lodger off on some vessel, pocketing his advance, which would amount to twenty or fifty dollars more, according to the length of the voyage for which he was shipped. Chase had heard much of landsharks from the sailors on board the Petrel, and he understood the situation perfectly, but he was at a loss how to get out of it. It would be folly to irritate the man, so he tried to appease him.

"There's no use in getting angry over it," said he. "What do you want me to do?"

"I want you to hand out your money, and let me take care of it for you," said the landlord.

"There it is," said Chase, producing the five-dollar bill.

"This ain't no account. We use gold in this country. Where's the rest? Better let me have it all, because I'm responsible, you know."

"You've got it all now. I haven't another cent."

"I don't believe it."

"Then you had better sound me," said Chase. "My wages amounted to only seventy-five dollars, and the articles I drew from the slop-chest used them all up."

"Well, you're a nice lad to come ashore after a long voyage, ain't you now?" said the landlord, who did not try to conceal his disgust.

"I am not worth robbing, am I?" said Chase, to himself.

"I believe you're a deserter," continued the landlord, "else you'd have more money."

"I couldn't very well have deserted in broad daylight with a bundle over my shoulder," said Chase. "And besides, there's my certificate of discharge."

"That may be all right, and then again it may not," said the landlord, holding the document upside down while he looked at it. "There's a law that governs us boarding-house keepers, and you must stay here till I find out whether or not you are all right."

"Very good," replied the boy, who knew that he could not help himself. "Send somebody down to the Petrel with that discharge, and if Captain Pratt doesn't say it is correct, I am willing to go back."

"Perhaps he'll put you in jail. That's what they do with deserters sometimes."

"I'll risk it. Now, if you will furnish me with writing materials, I'll write that letter. The sooner that money gets here, the better it will suit me."

"Will the old man be sure and send it?"

"Of course he will."

"Do you know anybody here in Fr'isco?"

"Not a soul."

"Then you had better tell him to send the money

to me—John McKay is my name—because you can't get it, being a stranger. You'll need somebody to prove who you be."

" Couldn't you do that?"

" Well, no; I couldn't. I don't know you from a side of sole leather. I never seen you before. If it is sent to me I can get it easy enough, no matter whether it comes by check or express."

." And then you can hand it over to me?"

" Of course, and I will, too—every cent. I'm honest."

" O, I don't doubt it," said Chase. "You look honest."

" Well, I'll go and get the pen, ink and paper for you, and then I'll show you to a room up-stairs, where you'll be quiet and peaceable like, and there won't be nobody to bother you."

" I can write the letter down here just as well," said Chase, who was afraid that if he went up-stairs he might not be allowed to come down again very soon, "and then I can take it to the post-office myself."

16

"But I don't want you to write it down here, because there's always fellows coming in. When you get it writ, I can send it to the office for you. Don't forget my name—John McKay."

"I won't," said Chase, rising to his feet. He executed this movement with the determination of making a bold strike for his freedom. The land-lord was moving toward the counter, and Chase stood ready for a spring, intending, as soon as he went behind it, to dart for the door and run out into the street. But the man acted as if he suspected his design, for he walked straight to the door, locked it and put the key into his pocket.

"That's just to keep everybody out till I come back," said he, by way of explanation.

The landlord then went behind his counter, and after overhauling the contents of a drawer, found the writing materials and a stamped envelope. Nodding to Chase to follow, he led the way out of the bar-room, up two flights of uncarpeted stairs, along a narrow, winding hall, and finally opened a door which led into a room so dark that Chase could not see a single thing in it. There were windows in it, however, for little streaks of light came in through what appeared to be closed blinds.

"Can't you give me a better room than this?" asked Chase, with an involuntary shudder. "I can't see to write in here."

"You can after a while," said the landlord. "It ain't so dark as it looks at first sight. Now, how long before I shall come back?"

"O, give me an hour. I've got a good deal to say, and besides it takes me a long time to write a letter."

The man deposited the writing materials on a rough table in one corner of the room, and then went out, closing the door after him, and turning a key in the lock as he did so. Chase heard it and knew that he was a prisoner.

CHAPTER XVI.

BROWN'S MISFORTUNE.

CHASE realized his situation, but he was not
as badly frightened as he would have been a
few months before. One soon learns to bear up
bravely under almost any adverse circumstances,
especially if he have an object in view. Chase had
an object to accomplish, and that was to reach home
and friends once more. He could do nothing
toward it while he was locked up there, so he at
once began an examination of his prison with a view
to escaping from it. He waited until the landlord
had descended the stairs, and then, after listening a
few minutes at the door, to make sure that he did
not come back, turned his attention to the nearest
window. He found there only the shattered remains of a sash, and what he had supposed to be

blinds were rough boards nailed on the outside. These boards were further secured by two bars of iron, one at the top and the other at the bottom. They had been forced out a little at the bottom, as far as the bar would allow them to go, and there were deep dents and scratches on them, showing that a lever of some kind had been used against them.

"This room is a regular jail," thought Chase. "That landlord takes in all the sailors that come here, and after they have spent every cent of their money, he locks them up here until he gets ready to ship them off on some vessel. That's what he intends to do with me, and he seems in a fair way to accomplish his object."

Talking thus to himself, Chase made a close examination of the fastenings of the window. Some one who had been confined in that room had made a desperate effort to push off the boards, that was evident, for the marks of the lever he had used were there yet. But before the boards could be pushed out far enough to draw the nails, they had been stopped by the bar outside. The first thing was to get at these nails and break them off. The bottom of one of the boards could then be pushed aside, leaving an opening through which he could crawl out.

Chase thought a moment, and then pulling out his knife, which fortunately contained a large, strong blade, set to work to cut through the soft wood of the window-sill, down to one of the nails which held the outside board. This he did in a very few minutes. Then he placed the point of his knife under the nail, and prying it up until he could take hold of it with his fingers, bent it back and forth until he broke it off. Three others were served in the same way, and then Chase pushed the lower end of the board aside and looked out. The roof of the adjoining house was six or eight feet lower than the window. It was flat, and there was a woman upon it engaged in hanging out clothes. She hung up the last article while Chase was looking at her, and picking up her empty

CHASE'S ESCAPE FROM THE SAILOR BOARDING-HOUSE.

basket disappeared through a scuttle which she left open behind her.

"I don't much like the situation," said the boy, wiping the big drops of perspiration from his face. "My only way of escape is through that house. Suppose that scuttle leads into the living-room of some family, and I should find a big fellow there who would want to know my business?"

Chase did not stop to answer this question, being resolved to trust to luck. He was working his way through the window while he was talking to himself, and hanging by his hands dropped down upon the roof. He ran at once to the scuttle, and upon looking into it, saw that it led into a hall which did not seem to be occupied. Without hesitation he descended the ladder, hurried down the flight of steps he found at the end of the hall, and in a moment more was safe in the street.

The very first man he saw when he got there was the landlord, John McKay, who stood in the open door of his boarding-house, no doubt looking out for an opportunity to take in some other unwary

sailor who had just landed from a long voyage.
If the boy's sudden appearance caused him any
surprise, he did not show it. He made no move,
and neither did he say anything. Chase walked
away, looking back now and then to make sure that
the landlord did not follow him, and at the first
corner he found a policeman, to whom he hurriedly
related all that had passed since his arrival at the
boarding-house. The officer did not act as though
he heard a word of the story. He kept looking up
and down the street, and when the boy ceased
speaking walked slowly toward the boarding-house,
Chase following. The landlord saw them coming,
but, somewhat to Chase's surprise, exhibited no
signs of alarm. He kept his place in the doorway,
and when the two came up, said, familiarly:

"Hallo, Jenkins!"

"How are you, Mack?" said the officer. "This
boy says you've got a bundle of his."

"Well, that isn't the only lie he's told since I
first seen him," returned the landlord. "He came
to my house about two weeks ago, without clothes or

money, and I've been boarding him free gratis ever since."

"Why, I came to your house not more than an hour ago, and you took my bundle away from me and robbed me of five dollars besides," said Chase, greatly amazed at the man's impudence.

"Do you hear that, Jim?" said the landlord, turning partly around and addressing some one in the house.

"I do," replied a voice; and a burly fellow, whom Chase had not before seen about the premises, came out from behind the bar and approached the door.   "That's the return you always get for doing a sailor-man a kindness.   I can show on the books that he owes for two weeks' board and lodging."

"I guess you had better move on," said the officer, turning to Chase.

"And leave my clothes and money?   I guess not.   They're mine and I want them.   I make a complaint against this man, and it is your business to arrest him."

"Go on without another word," said the police-man, "or I'll make it my business to run you in."

Chase was not a city boy, but he knew what the officer meant. Filled with surprise and bewilder-ment, he turned about and made his way around a corner, out of sight. When he reached the next street he looked back, and saw that the policeman was standing on the corner watching him.

"Now I am beaten," thought Chase, turning down the first street he came to, in order to leave the hated officer out of sight. " A landshark robs me in broad daylight, and a policeman upholds him in it, and threatens to arrest me if I say another word! I wonder if that is what city folks call justice!"

Chase lost heart now, for the only time since his first night on board the Petrel. With no clothing or money, alone in a strange city, where the officers appeared to be in league with the rascals, and an honest boy was followed and watched as if he were a suspicious character, it was no wonder that he felt afraid and dispirited. He did not dare remain in

San Francisco now, for if, while in search of employment, he should chance to wander back on policeman Jenkins's beat, that officer might arrest him and have him locked up as a vagrant. The bare thought was horrifying to Chase, who hurried along as if he hoped to get away from it, turning down every corner he came to, until at last he found himself near the wharf again. Here he was accosted by a stalwart young fellow with a pack on his back, who hurriedly asked if a boat, which was lying close by with steam up, was the one that carried passengers from Fr'isco to Vallejo.

"I am sure I don't know," answered Chase. "I am a stranger here. Where is Vallejo?"

"It is on the other side of the bay," replied the man. "It is the place where they go to take the cars for the States."

"Then I should like to go there," said Chase, eagerly. "I am bound for the States."

"So am I, if I can ever get there. I came out here three years ago to dig gold, and I had more money when I first got here than I have ever had since.

I shall never be able to scrape enough together to pay my fare to Indiana, so I am going to work my way back. They want hands on the railroad up here at Independence. They are paying three dollars a day."

"Now, I should like a chance like that," said Chase. "Where is Independence?"

"Up the road a piece."

"How is one to get there?"

"That's the question. If we were only at Vallejo, we could walk up the railroad; but there are twenty-five miles of water between us and that place."

"Well, won't the railroad company furnish transportation to those who want to work for them?"

"I don't know. Suppose we go back and look."

Chase did not know what the man meant by going back and looking, but he followed him without asking any questions, and presently found himself in front of a large placard posted on a billboard and headed—

"500 *More Men Wanted to Work on the Central Pacific Railroad.*"

It was this notice that had first put it into the head of Chase's new acquaintance to work his way back to his home in Indiana; and near the bottom was something that had escaped his eye:

"*For further particulars and transportation, apply at the Company's Office, No. 54 K street, Sacramento.*"

"Humph! we are no better off now than we were before," said Chase, who remembered enough of his geography to know that Sacramento was some distance from San Francisco. "How are we ever going to get to the company's office."

"Go right aboard that steamer you see up there," said a man, who was standing near enough to them to overhear their conversation. "She goes to Vallejo, and from there you can take the train to Sacramento."

"Without a cent in our pockets?" asked Chase's companion.

"Yes, if you will contract to work on the railroad for one month."

"*I* will, and be glad of the chance," said Chase. "We are obliged to you for the information."

Chase and his friend hurried back to the steamer, and going on board seated themselves near a group of men who were congregated on the lower deck. They were rough-looking fellows, of all nationalities, and as many of them were talking earnestly in their own tongue—although nobody appeared to be listening to them—the hubbub that arose made Chase wonder. Like himself, they were bound for the company's office; and he shovelled dirt and blasted rocks in company with some of them for many a day afterward.

During the run up the bay Chase told his new friend, who said his name was George Brown, something of his history, and in return Brown gave him a sketch of his own life. It did not take him long to do it, for he had nothing interesting or exciting to tell. He had left a comfortable home in the States, hoping to acquire a fortune in a few days in California. He had gone first to the mines, and, although he had seen men take gold in paying quantities from holes almost by the side of the one in which he was working, he had not been able to earn enough to pay for his provisions. He had finally become a teamster, and on more than one occasion had been glad to saw wood for his breakfast. He was bound to get home now in some way, and when he once got there he would stay. If he had worked half as hard on his farm as he had worked in California for the last three years, he would have had money in the bank.

The trip up the bay would, no doubt, have been a pleasant one to Chase had he been in a frame of mind to enjoy it. But he was thinking of his home off in Louisiana, and of his friends, who now seemed farther away from him than ever before. If this man, who was accustomed to work and to "roughing it," had been three years trying to get back to his home, how long at that rate would it take *him*, Chase asked himself.

When the steamer reached Vallejo he followed the others to the train, and was packed away in a box-car for Sacramento. At the company's office

he went through certain forms of agreement, which
he could not have repeated when he came out if he
had tried, and was then ordered into another box-
car that was to take him to Independence. He
travelled night and day, and, although he had no
bed to sleep on, he had plenty to eat, and kept up
his spirits by telling himself over and over again
that every turn of the wheels brought him nearer
to his home.

Arriving at Independence, he was put to work at
once, and during the next month led a life of toil
and hardship to which his experience on board the
Petrel was mere boy's play. The first thing he
did when he had a few minutes' leisure, was to hunt
up the superintendent, or the " boss," as the men
called him, to whom he stated his troubles, and of
whom he begged a stamped envelope, and a sheet
of paper, and borrowed a lead-pencil. With these
he wrote a long letter to his father, telling what he
had done since leaving Bellville and what he intended to do, not forgetting to mention the amount
which he thought would be necessary to take him

home ; and having given the letter into the hands of the superintendent, who promised to see that it was duly sent off, he went to work with a lighter heart than he had carried for many a day, believing that by the time his month had expired, the assistance he so much needed would be at hand.

"And when it does come, Brown," said Chase, who had learned to look upon his new acquaintance with almost a brother's affection, " you shall not be left out in the cold. If it hadn't been for you I wouldn't be here now, and I'll see you through as far as my money will take us."

It was well for the boy's peace of mind that he did not know what became of that letter. The superintendent put it carefully away in his pocket, and took it out again—nearly eight weeks afterward, when the one who wrote it was hopelessly lost in the mountains near Fort Bolton.

Although Chase expected a happy deliverance out of all his troubles without any effort on his part to bring it about, neither he nor Brown neglected to post himself in everything that it might be neces-

sary for them to know, in case they should be com-
pelled to continue their journey without money to
pay their fare on the stages.   Among other things,
they learned that the Union Pacific, which was
slowly advancing to meet the road on which they
were at work, had progressed beyond Cheyenne, and
that between that point and Independence there
were several trails and stage-routes, some longer and
some shorter, but any one of which would lead them
in the direction they wished to go.   Their fellow-
workmen assured them that it would not be much
of a tramp across the country for a couple of healthy
youngsters, and if at any time they got out of food,
the first man they met would be willing to supply
them, no matter whether they had money or not.

The month for which Chase and his friend had
contracted wore slowly away, but the expected letter
from Bellville did not arrive.   Chase grew more and
more impatient and anxious as the days passed, and
when he was paid off at the end of the month, he
would have been glad to renew his contract, but
Brown would not listen.   "Let's put out and go to

work when we reach the other road," said he.
"You can write to your father just as well from
Cheyenne as you can from here.   Your letter must
have miscarried."

Brown emphasized his advice by declaring that
he was going whether Chase did or not.   Cold
weather was coming on, he said ; the snow had fallen,
during the previous winter, sixty feet deep over
seven miles of the road-bed on which the rails had
since been laid, and he did not like the idea of being
shut out from home by any such barrier as that.
He was bound to get through to the other side of
the mountains before winter set in, come what might.
So Chase reluctantly made up the small bundle of
clothing and bedding he had purchased from the
stores, put carefully away the slender stock of money
that he had remaining after paying his board-bill
and other debts he had contracted, and followed
Brown, who stepped off with a light heart.   The
latter's face was turned toward home once more,
and that was enough to put him in the best of
spirits.

"If we were in the settlements now," said he, making an effort to bring Chase's usual smile back to his face, "the folks would say of us: 'Look at those two tramps; lock the dog in the hen-house.' But out here, where there are better fellows than ourselves as poor as we, we are 'emigrants,' and people don't think it necessary to watch us, lest we should steal everything they've got."

Keeping up a fire of small-talk, Brown enlivened many a mile of their first day's journey, and finally succeeded in making his companion take a brighter view of their prospects. They made about twenty miles by dark, and then built a fire beside the road and went into camp.

Chase awoke once during the night and saw Brown sitting by the fire, engaged in tying his money up in his handkerchief. He simply noted the fact, and would never have thought of it again, had it not been brought to his mind by an incident that happened the next day. They were walking along toward the close of the afternoon, when Brown, who had kept up a constant singing and story-telling, suddenly paused and put his hand into his pocket. He opened his eyes, felt in his other pocket, then threw down his bundle and began a thorough examination of his clothing.

"What's the matter?" asked Chase.

"Matter enough," replied his companion, glancing back along the road. "I've lost my money."

CHAPTER XVII.

WHAT CAME OF IT.

YES, sir, I have lost my money," repeated Brown, pulling out each of his pockets in succession, to show that they were all empty. "I haven't got a red cent."

"But it wasn't in your pocket," said Chase, as soon as he had recovered from his surprise.

"Eh?" exclaimed Brown, his face assuming a genuine look of astonishment now. "How do you know it wasn't?"

"Because I saw you sitting by the fire last night, tying your money up in your handkerchief," replied Chase.

"Ah! I—eh? Yes; certainly you did, and that very move was what has ruined me. Money, handkerchief and all are gone."

Chase looked sharply at his companion. There

was something about the business that did not look just right. Brown didn't act sorry enough.

"I say it is gone," said the latter, as if Chase had disputed the point. "What is to be done now? You'll have to support us both, Hank."

"But fifteen dollars will not buy us food until we reach Cheyenne," replied Chase.

"I know it; but it will have to last us as long as we can make it, and then we must go to work. If we can find nothing to do, the only thing left for us is to separate and let each fellow take care of himself."

Again Chase looked closely at his friend. This was a new doctrine for the latter to advocate. Heretofore, especially since he learned that Chase expected assistance from home, Brown had laid great stress on the fact that they were to remain together until they reached the States, no matter what might happen; and if good fortune befell either of them, the other was to share it. Chase had been glad to agree to it. As matters stood when they left Independence, Brown had the advantage, for not having been obliged to purchase any clothes or bedding, he had been able to save every cent of his month's wages, except what he had expended for food. If the superintendent had mailed that letter, then Chase would have carried the heavier purse, and he never would have thought of deserting his companion.

"I never saw the like of this," said Brown, looking down at the ground and shaking his head.

"We'll not give it up without trying to find it," said Chase. "Let's go back."

With a great show of eagerness Brown caught up his bundle and hurried down the road, followed by Chase, who, however, did not make any effort to find the money. He had found it already. He could have put his hand upon it without stepping out of his tracks. The moment Brown turned his back to him, he saw something sticking out from under the collar of his shirt. It was the corner of a blue cotton handkerchief—the same one in which Chase had seen him tying up his money the night before. The gold was slung around Brown's neck, under his shirt. Of that much Chase was certain; but he was not quite so certain that he understood the motive the man had in view in hiding it.

"I don't think there is any need of going farther back," said Brown, pausing and looking dejectedly at Chase, after they had retraced their steps for a short distance up the road; "do you?"

"No, I do not," answered the boy. "We have travelled fast to-day, and it is a long way back to the place where we camped last night. You had the money then?"

"Yes, and I haven't seen it since. Some fellow has got it safe enough before this time."

"I know it," said Chase.

With one accord the two turned about and resumed their journey. Chase wanted to think, but Brown was anxious to talk.

"What do you say to my proposition, Hank?" said he. "I don't like to leave you, but if we can't get work together, ought not each one to look out for himself?"

"Of course he ought."

"But you won't leave me in the lurch?" continued Brown. "You won't go back on me because I have no money?"

"I have just as much intention of deserting you as you have of serving me that way," replied Chase, earnestly.

"Give me your hand on that, my boy," said Brown. "I knew you were true blue, or I shouldn't have stuck to you as long as I have."

Brown, having, as he imagined, extorted a promise from his companion that he would remain with him as long as his money held out, relapsed into silence, and the boy was allowed leisure to follow out some plans that had suggested themselves to him. In the first place, he wanted to make sure that he was not mistaken in regard to the money; so he watched his opportunity, and presently he and Brown bumped their shoulders together with some violence, as people will sometimes do who walk together without keeping step. The result was positive proof that Brown had not lost his money, for Chase heard the gold pieces jingle as plainly as he could hear the sound of his own footsteps. Brown heard it, too, and glanced quickly into Chase's face; but seeing nothing there to excite his suspicions, he said nothing, but simply moved farther away so that the experiment could not be repeated.

"The money is tied up in his handkerchief, just as I supposed it was," soliloquized Chase. "I think I begin to see into the matter a little. We have just fifty-five dollars between us—I have fifteen and he owns the balance,—and that must last us during a tramp of nearly four hundred miles. He thinks that forty dollars will furnish food for one man longer than fifty-five will for two. He intends to live off my money without touching his own, and when I am strapped, he is going to run away from me; and he'll have his forty dollars left to support him during the rest of his journey. It is enough for one, but I am a good deal of his opinion that it is not enough for two. Now, fifteen dollars will keep me alone in food longer than it will both of us, so if you please, Mr. Brown, *I'll* do the running away myself.   If I must travel on my own hook, I'll do it while I have money in my pocket."

Chase had hit the nail squarely on the head.   He had told Brown's plans in detail as well as Brown could have told them himself.   The truth of the matter was, that the man was too homesick to be either honest or truthful.   He was determined to work his way back to Indiana by some means, no matter who might suffer by it.

"I have half a mind to tell him that I know what he is about," thought Chase.   "The coward, to want to desert me when I offered to give him half the money I expected to receive from father! I say, Brown!"

When the boy had said this much, prudence stepped in, and he paused.   If he excited Brown's anger, the latter might take his money away from him by force, and then he would be in a predicament indeed.

"Well, what is it?" asked Brown.   "Bad business, ain't it?"

" Yes, it is," replied Chase. " How long do you suppose my fifteen dollars will last us?"

" We must make it hold out as long as we possibly can, even if we eat but one full meal a day. But there is no use in looking so down-hearted over it. We'll work through somehow."

Brown broke out into a song, to show how lightly the matter sat on his own mind, and Chase once more went off into a reverie. During the rest of the day he had little to say, and when night came he made preparations to slip away from his companion; but no opportunity offered itself. Did Brown suspect his designs? He certainly acted as if he did, for he kept a sharp eye on Chase all the time. If the latter moved during the night, Brown turned over and looked at him.

For the three following days and nights Chase lived under a sort of surveillance that was galling to him, and during that time the provisions they had brought with them from Independence were exhausted, and two of Chase's fifteen dollars were spent at Salt Lake City, to replenish their store.

On the fourth night they encamped near a party of teamsters. Brown being weary with the day's journey remained at the fire, while Chase started out to pay a visit to their neighbors. They were glad to see him, offered him some of their supper, and, of course, wanted to know where he was going and what he intended to do when he got there. Chase answered all their questions, and in accordance with his usual custom, made inquiries concerning the route to Cheyenne. The teamsters being perfectly familiar with the road gave him all the information he asked, and then one of them said :

"If you only knew it, you are going miles out of your way by going to Cheyenne. Why don't you take the other trail?"

"Where is it?" asked Chase.

"About a quarter of a mile below here. It is the first road that turns to your right. You can't miss it, for there is a big dead oak hanging over it. You'll save at least a hundred miles of hard walking by taking that route, and you'll strike the prairie either at Bolton or Reynolds. When you get there, you will be just as near the States as you will be at Cheyenne."

"Any chance of losing my way?"

"Not if you keep your eyes open and use your tongue."

"What can I find to eat?"

"Just as much as you can by this route. You'll meet a team or a train every day."

"Any grizzly bears or other ferocious animals on the way?"

"No more than there are on this. There's plenty of grouse, and if you get hard up for grub, you can snare and cook enough in a day to last you a week. I was lost down in there once, years ago, when the trail wasn't as well travelled as it is now, and, although I had nothing but a pocket-knife with me, I lived on the fat of the land and had a good time besides."

The teamster then went on to relate the particulars of his adventure, which did not have much interest for Chase, for he was thinking of something else. When the story was finished, he bade his entertainers good-night, and slowly returned to his own camp. Now was the time, he told himself, to put his plans into execution. A lonely journey through the mountains was not a pleasant thing to look forward to, but it was better than remaining in company with a man who intended to live off him as long as his money held out, and then desert him. He would take his bundle and start off on his own hook that very night.

Having come to this determination, Chase made the best of his way back to his camp, walking with noiseless footsteps, so as not to disturb Brown, who, he supposed, must be asleep by this time. But his precaution proved to be useless, for Brown was wide awake and waiting for him. "I thought you were never coming back," said he, with some impatience.

"Those fellows down there had some very interesting stories to tell," replied Chase. "Say, Brown, would you sell your pack for ten dollars, if you were me?"

"Ten dollars!" exclaimed Brown, raising himself on his elbow, "I guess I would. That would buy lots of bacon and biscuit."

"I could use one of your blankets at night, couldn't I?" added Chase.

"Of course you can, as long as we remain together."

"Then that settles it."

As Chase said this, he caught up his bundle and hurried down the road again, while Brown lay back in his blanket to await his return, laughing to himself when he thought how nicely he was taking care of himself at the expense of his confiding friend. He waited an hour, but Chase did not return; still another, and then he got up and walked down the road. When he came within sight of the camp of the teamsters he saw that the fire was burning brightly, but the men themselves were wrapped up in their blankets, sleeping soundly. Nothing more being needed to convince him that a very neat trick had been played upon him, Brown turned and walked back to his own fire.

Meanwhile Chase was hurrying along the old

trail to which the teamster had directed him. He had no difficulty in finding it, for the dead oak tree pointed out its location. It was very dark and gloomy in there, for the mountains on both sides were thickly covered with trees, and the rays of the moon could scarcely penetrate through the dense shade which they threw over the road. The road itself, however, showed very plainly through the darkness, and Chase had no difficulty in following it. He travelled with all the speed of which he was capable until too tired to go farther; and then building a fire beside the road, he lay down near it and slept until morning.

Ere many days had passed away Chase found that he could get on just as well without Brown as he had done with him. He met any number of teamsters and emigrants, who willingly answered his questions concerning the route before him, and if he happened on a camp during the dinner or supper hour, he was cordially invited to "stop and take a bite." Of course he was always obliged to tell his story to those whose hospitality he shared, and when he departed, he was invariably provided with all the cooked provisions he was willing to carry in addition to his bundle, and they never cost him a cent. At that rate his thirteen dollars would last him until he reached home. Of course, too, the journey grew more and more monotonous and wearisome as the days passed, and, worse than all, the thick, strong shoes he had purchased before leaving Independence, began to show signs of wear. But just as they were ready to drop to pieces, he met a kind-hearted emigrant, who gave him a pair of old boots, which, although much too large for him, served to keep his feet off the hard, rocky road. It was getting colder, too, every day; the leaves were falling from the trees, the wind whistled dismally through the gorges, the teams and wagon-trains were not as often met us at first, and everything told Chase that winter was fast approaching. "You'd better toddle along right peert," said one of the teamsters to him. "Bolton, which is the nighest station, is two hundred and fifty miles away yet, and we're going to ketch it in a few days. When she does come she'll be a snorter.

You've got a good stretch of prairie to cross after you leave the foot-hills, and you don't want to get ketched out there in a snow-storm. Look out for that."

Chase gave heed to the friendly warning, and made headway as rapidly as possible. "Two hundred and fifty miles," he kept saying to himself. His journey was not half completed, and it seemed to him that he had been an age on the road. Would he ever reach Bolton? Sometimes he was almost ready to give up trying, and lie down in the road and wait until the snows of winter came and covered him up. Then recollections of home and friends would come thronging upon him, and he would press forward with renewed energy, in spite of blistered feet and weary, aching limbs, which sometimes almost refused to sustain him. He was up before the sun, and continued his journey until long after dark. His situation at best was bad enough, but one night he met with an adventure that made it infinitely worse.

As he was hurrying along after dark, he came

suddenly upon a camp-fire. He was glad to see it, for he had not met a human being for the last three days, and the provisions that had been furnished him by the last teamster were all exhausted. He hoped to procure a fresh supply at this camp. If he could not, he would be obliged to spend a day or two in trapping grouse; and he was so very much afraid of the snow-storm which had been so often predicted, that he did not dare to waste a single hour. Furthermore, the road of late had been growing very rough and rocky, and he could no longer see the prints of wagon-wheels. He began to fear that while travelling in the dark, he had lost his way. Perhaps these people could set him right. He walked boldly up to the fire and greeted the men sitting there—two rough-looking fellows, whom he at once put down as hunters.

"Good evening, strangers," said he.

"Wal, what do you want?" growled one of the men, after they had both given him a good looking over.

"Will you give me some supper and permission

to sleep by your fire?" asked Chase, rather doubt-fully. This was the first time during his fifteen days in the mountains that any one had spoken to him so roughly.

"I don't reckon we've got any more grub nor we want ourselves," was the surly response.

"O, I don't ask you to give it to me," said Chase. "I am able and willing to pay for it."

"You got any shiners?" asked the hunter, running his eyes over the boy's clothes.

"I know I don't look like it, but I can prove my words. See there," said Chase, putting his hand into his pocket and drawing out several gold and silver pieces.

"How many of them you got?"

"Thirteen dollars' worth. Can you give me something to eat now?"

"I reckon we mought," said the man, pointing to a haunch of venison that hung upon a tree close by.

Having become accustomed to the ways of the world, Chase understood the invitation thus given.

He took down the joint, cut off a couple of generous slices with his knife, and holding them over the flames with two sticks, looked about him with some satisfaction. His supper was secure ; he had a warm fire to sleep by, and that was something on which to congratulate himself.

The men were hunters or trappers, sure enough, Chase told himself, and as they were the first of their calling he had ever seen, he looked at them with as much curiosity as the Sportsman's Club had looked at Parks and Reed, when those worthies first came into their camp. They wore buckskin coats and moccasins, were armed with rifles, and there were two bundles of furs, principally otter and beaver-skins, near the fire. They had no blankets, but each had a saddle for a pillow, and their horses were picketed on the other side of the road. In answer to an inquiry from Chase, they told him, rather gruffly, that they had been hunting in the mountains, and were on their way to some fort to dispose of their plunder. They did not seem inclined to talk. They smoked their pipes and watched the boy while he ate his supper, growled out a reply in the affirmative when he asked if he was on the road to Fort Bolton, but paid no attention to the pleasant good-night he wished them as he rolled himself up in his blankets preparatory to going to sleep.

That was the last comfortable night that Chase passed for more than a week.

CHAPTER XVIII.

CONCLUSION.

CHASE was awakened the next morning by the crackling of the fire which the hunters had replenished at daylight. He started up with a cheery "good-morning" on his lips, but no sooner was he fairly awake, than a sight caught his eyes which arrested the words ere they were spoken. The men, having finished their breakfast, were overhauling his bundle—or rather one of them was, while the other sat by smoking his pipe and looking at him. Chase found, too, that the blanket which had covered him during the night, had been pulled off, and was now rolled up and tied to the horn of one of the saddles.

"I am to be robbed, I can see that plainly enough," said Chase, his heart sinking within him.

" I have been afraid of it all along, and it has come at last.   I might as well give up now.   But if I am to lose all my things, I'll at least have a breakfast in part payment," he added, after a moment's reflection.

The men looked at Chase as he got up, but did not speak to him.   He took down the haunch of venison, and while he was cutting off a portion of it, the hunter who was examining his bundle, coolly rolled up the blanket from which he had just arisen, and laid it down beside his saddle.   Chase shivered as he watched the operation, and thought of the nights he had yet to pass in the mountains, but said nothing.   He thrust some sticks through the slices of venison, and proceeded to roast them over the flames.

" Now, then," said the hunter, who had done the most of the talking the night before, " whar's them shiners ?"

Chase, holding his breakfast with one hand, emptied his pocket with the other, giving up his hard-earned wages without a word of remonstrance.

"Be these all you've got?" asked the man.

"Every cent. If you don't believe it, you can go through me."

The man took him at his word, turning all his pockets inside out, passing his hand around his neck to make sure that he did not carry a purse suspended beneath his shirt, and even feeling of the seams of his trowsers and jacket. Having satisfied himself that the boy had told the truth, he ordered him to pull off his boots. Chase obeyed, shaking each one as he did so, to show that there was nothing in it.

"O, I know you hain't got no more money," said the man, impatiently. "Hand them boots here. They're too big for you, an' mebbe they'll fit me."

"Now you are not barbarian enough to turn me adrift in this wilderness at this time of the year barefooted, are you?" cried Chase, in great alarm.

"You cook that grub o' your'n, an' let it stop

your mouth; that's the best thing you can do," was the reply.

Chase thought so too. The savage look on the man's face frightened him, and he told himself that he would not object again, no matter what they did to him.

The hunter pulled off his moccasins and proceeded to draw on Chase's boots, which, contrary to the boy's hopes, fitted him as if they had been made for him. He grunted out his satisfaction, and picking up his moccasins was about to toss them to Chase, when his companion interposed. "Hand 'em here," said he. "I reckon I can use 'em as well as anybody."

The hunter accordingly passed the moccasins to his friend, who drew them on over his own, and Chase settled back on the ground with a despairing sigh. He was to be left barefooted, sure enough.

The men having appropriated every article of value that Chase possessed (fortunately they did not think his pocket-knife and the contents of his bundle worth stealing), brought up their horses, and while one put the saddles on them, the other employed himself in gathering their luggage together, not even forgetting what remained of the haunch of venison, which Chase hoped they would leave behind them. When all was ready for the start, they mounted and one rode off at once, while the other stopped to say a parting word to the boy. "No follerin' now," he exclaimed, savagely. "If we set eyes on you agin, you won't get off so easy."

The hunter then rode on after his companion, and Chase was left alone. So stunned and bewildered was he that he could scarcely realize his situation. Hardly knowing what he was about, he replenished the fire, cooked and ate his slices of venison, and then picking up the only extra shirt he possessed, set to work to cut it into strips, so that he could make of it some protection for his feet. He could not stay there and starve while he had the strength to move, and neither could he travel barefooted over those frosty stones. Having wrapped up his feet as well as he could, he bundled up his clothes and resumed his journey.

In after life, Chase was never able to tell just

what happened during the two weeks following the night he spent in the hunters' camp. He knew that he lived through them, and that was all he did know. During all this time he was lost—there was not a road or a path to be found anywhere. While daylight lasted he picked his way wearily over logs and rocks and through tangled thickets, and at night sat beside his lonely fire, shivering with the cold and thinking of home. Fortunately he had a flint and steel and an abundance of tinder, and fortunately, too, grouse were plenty and he knew how to snare them, so that he never suffered for want of food. The clothing in his bundle was gradually used up for protection for his feet, and he had not yet been able to make up his mind what he would do when the last piece was gone.

One day he found himself standing on the brink of a precipice overlooking a valley, about ten miles in circumference. In attempting to work his way to the bottom he missed his footing and fell, bruising himself severely and tearing his clothing almost into shreds. He had a roasted grouse in each hand, to which he held fast; and when he had rested a few minutes, leaning against the boulder which had stopped him in his descent, he arose and struggled forward again. After some trouble he succeeded in finding an outlet to the valley, which was a rocky gorge running between lofty mountains. He camped in the mouth of this gorge, and on the afternoon of the next day found himself within sight of the prairie. His hopes rose a moment, and then sank to zero again. There were no more mountains and gullies to be passed, but there was many a mile of prairie to be traversed, and he was in just as much danger of being hopelessly bewildered and lost, as he had been at any time during his journey. While he was thinking about it, he came suddenly around a tall rock, which jutted out into the gorge like a promontory into the ocean, and was brought to a stand-still by an unexpected sight. A drove of horses were on the point of entering the gorge. They were close upon him, and Chase, to save himself from being run down by them, sprang quickly behind the nearest tree. The horses saw him and swerved from their course, and at the same time Chase heard some words addressed to him by a horseman who was riding in the rear of the drove. He was sure the words were addressed to him, for the horseman looked straight toward him, and, more than that, he raised his hand and shook something at him. It was the first time for many a long day that Chase had heard the sound of a human voice, but it was not a welcome sound, for he thought he recognised the horseman. It was one of the hunters who had robbed him. Remembering the parting threat they had uttered, Chase turned and retreated up the hill with all possible speed. Before he reached the top he heard the horses rushing down the gorge, and then the sound of voices came to his ears. No doubt the hunters believed that he had followed them, and were about to hunt him up and do something terrible to him. Frightened at the thought, Chase crept away and hid himself in a hollow log, from which he never ventured out again until long after dark.

The week following this incident was another

memorable one to the wanderer. He was lost again. The mountains were full of gullies, which crossed and recrossed one another in every direction, and he could not find the prairie. He knew which way he ought to go, for the sun told him; but none of the gullies ran that way, and their sides were much too steep to be scaled. Turn which way he would, nothing but rocks and stunted trees met his gaze.

Finally the last bone of the last grouse he had snared was picked clean and thrown away, and for the first time Chase began to suffer from the pangs of hunger. That same day, too, something came which he had long been dreading—a snow-storm. It was wonderful how rapidly it increased in violence when it was once fairly started! The wind which roared up the gorges could not have been colder if it had come off some of the icebergs he had seen in going around Cape Horn, and he had never in his life seen so much snow as he saw during the next few hours. Drifts began to show themselves. Some of them were a foot or more in depth, and when Chase waded through them, he felt the snow settling around his bare ankles. That took all the courage out of him.

"I don't know what I shall do now," said he, almost ready to abandon himself to despair. "I'm snowed up. It will be of no use for me to try to find the prairie now, for I would not dare go out there; and if I stay here——"

Chase suddenly stopped, faced quickly about and made an effort to take to his heels, but the bundle of cloths which he wore on his feet impeded his progress, tripped him up and he went down in a snow-drift. Scrambling up with all possible haste, he wiped the snow out of his eyes, and took a survey of the objects that had excited his alarm. There was no one in sight; but there was a smouldering fire under the cliffs, two wagons in the road, one with a broken axletree, two mules lying dead in the harness, an ox lying dead in his yoke, and the remains of another, which had been butchered, close by him. There were plenty of footprints about, and the persons who made them could not have been long absent, for the snow, which constantly sifted down from the bluffs above, had not yet filled them entirely up.

"They're gone!" said Chase, looking all around, "and even if they should come back and should prove to be enemies, they could not have the heart to refuse me something to eat. The men who robbed me gave me a supper and breakfast."

Encouraged by these thoughts, Chase drew near and looked into both the wagons, examined the footprints, to see whether those who made them were white men or Indians, and then raking the coals together and blowing them into a blaze with his hat, piled on some wood that happened to be lying near, and went to the slaughtered ox to select a piece of meat for his dinner.

"Something is always happening just in the nick of time," said Chase, as he turned the piece of meat before the fire. "My affairs may take a turn for the better yet. I noticed a pair of boots in one of those wagons—pretty well worn, it is true, but much better than what I have been wearing during the last three weeks, and also some clothing that will perhaps be more comfortable than this I have on. I hope the owners will not return until I have had time to make a selection from their store. It is always darkest just before daylight."

Yes, and Chase's day was just on the point of dawning. While he was talking thus with himself, the sound of footsteps in the snow caused him to look up in alarm. There was a party approaching, but there was nothing in the appearance of those who composed it to induce Chase to flee from them. He felt more like running to meet them. The new-comers were the Pike and his family. The old man led the way with a bundle thrown over his shoulder, and a child on each arm. He seemed surprised to see Chase, but was as profuse in his offers of hospitality as he had been when Archie Winters and his two companions first entered his camp.

"How do, stranger?" said he, cheerfully. "Making yourself to home, eh? That's right. It hain't much we've got to offer now, but you're as welcome as the flowers of May."

" Is this your property, sir ?" asked the boy.

" Yes, and it is all I have left of what I brought with me from the States."

" You have met with an accident ?"

" Yes, and been robbed !"

" By Indians ?"

" No ; by white men !"

" I was served the same way," said Chase, in alarm. " I hope they have gone away."

" O, yes. They've taken all that is worth stealing, and there is no fear that they will come back. But they left me this," said the Pike, patting his bundle as he placed it carefully on the ground, " and I can soon replace what I have lost. I've got a million dollars here."

" Why, I should think they would have taken it from you," said Chase, looking doubtfully at the man and wondering if he was in his right mind.

" It would have been of no use to them—that's the reason they didn't take it."

Chase glanced at the Pike's wife and children, who ranged themselves on the opposite side of the

fire without saying a word, and then turned his
attention to the man himself, who began undoing
his bundle, finally disclosing to view the machine
which was to run his quartz-mill when he reached
his gold-mine in the mountains. Chase, unable to
make out what it was, asked some questions concerning it, but the Pike was too busy to reply.
Reuben, with whom he next tried to be sociable,
didn't want to talk or didn't know how; but the
woman had a tongue and it was a matter of no
difficulty to set it going.

While Chase was eating his meat, and listening
to her story of the adventures that had lately befallen
herself and family, another party approached the
camp-fire—three boys about Chase's own age, who
came plodding along through the snow with bundles
thrown over their shoulders. They looked at Chase
in great amazement, and one of them said, in a voice
which he meant should be audible only to his companions, but whose shrill, piping tones nevertheless
reached the wanderer's ear and set his heart to
beating like a trip-hammer—

"Hallo! who is this stranger, and where did the Pike pick him up?"

The boys behind looked over their leader's shoulder to see who the stranger was, and Chase heard one of them exclaim: "I declare, that's the Wild Man of the Woods, fellows! He's the one who frightened the horses!"

As the three boys drew nearer Chase's heart continued to beat loudly, and his eyes began to open with amazement. He looked again and again, brushing away a mist that appeared to obstruct his vision, and then sat as motionless as if he had been turned into one of the boulders that lay scattered around. He noticed, too, that something created a commotion among the approaching boys. The one in front uttered an exclamation that quickly brought the one in the rear to his side, and the two stood looking first at Chase, then at each other, and whispering eagerly. At length one of them called out abruptly:

"Say, fellow, who are you?"

"O, Eugene!" was all poor Chase could say.

He had borne up bravely so far, but he could bear up no longer. To hear the tones of a familiar and kindly voice out there in that wilderness, when he had thought himself a thousand miles from everybody he had ever seen or heard of, was too much for the wanderer in his demoralized condition. He leaned his hands upon his knees, buried his face in them and sobbed convulsively.

"It *is* Hank, as sure as the world!" cried both Fred and Eugene, in tones which showed that they were not quite ready to believe it after all.

They dropped their bundles, and hurrying up to the long lost boy threw themselves down one on each side of him. "Look up, Hank," said Eugene, "and let us see if it is really you. Speak to a fellow, can't you?"

But Chase could neither look up nor speak. His tears flowed freely as he rocked himself back and forth on the ground. His two friends glanced at his tattered clothing, at the rags which covered his feet, then at his blue cold hands, and the eyes they raised to Archie Winters's astonished face were not dry by any means. Fred nodded his head toward one of the bundles, and Archie understanding the sign, quickly untied it, and handed out a pair of blankets which Fred and Eugene threw over Chase's shivering form, and then patiently waited for him to speak, resting their arms over his shoulders meanwhile, as if to assure him of their protection.

"He is a friend of ours," said Featherweight, in answer to an inquiring look from the Pike and his wife. "He lives near us in Louisiana, and used to go to school with us."

"Well, I do think in my soul!" cried the worthy couple, in concert.

"Yes. The last time we saw him was in Cuba, and how he ever came out here is a mystery."

And of course it remained a mystery until Chase was ready to explain, which he did as soon as he was warmed up both inside and out. A cup of hot coffee (fortunately there proved to be enough of the coffee-pot left to serve the purpose for which it was originally intended), a roaring fire, the substitution of a pair of stockings and boots for the insufficient protection his feet had known during the last few days, and, better than all, the knowledge that he was among friends again, worked a wonderful change in the wanderer. Every one about the fire listened eagerly while he related the story of his trials, and when he concluded, Eugene told what had happened to the Sportsman's Club since they had last seen Chase in Cuba; so that it was long after midnight before a wink of sleep was had about that fire by any but the Pike's children.

Hemlock boughs for beds and wood for the fire were plenty ; so were blankets, such as they were ; the overhanging cliff protected them from the storm ; and Chase once more slept soundly and without suffering from the cold. The next day the boys all went out to the mouth of the gorge to see if there were any signs of their friends, and Archie added that sentence to the notice he had already written on the beech tree. It would have been nearer correct had he written it : " Chase has found us."

The very next day the looked-for help arrived, and then there was a jubilee indeed ! Chase's story had to be told all over again, and it lost nothing in the telling, for those who had already heard it were just as much interested in it as were the new-comers. No less interesting to Frank, Walter and the rest of the Club, was the history of the exploits that Archie and his two companions had performed since leaving Fort Bolton.   They had actually succeeded in capturing the wild horse, and it was through no fault or mismanagement of their own that they had lost him.   Of course everybody sympathized with them, and Archie was the hero of the hour.

The storm abated that night, and early the next morning preparations were made to return to the Fort.   Dick and old Bob superintended the work, and in a very short space of time their horses, which had never worn a collar before, were harnessed to the uninjured wagon; and when Chase, and the Pike and all his belongings, had been put into it, the journey was commenced.   It lasted four days, but the travellers enjoyed themselves in spite of the cold weather that set in after the storm.

Chase remained at the Fort only one day—just long enough to provide himself with suitable clothing; and when Uncle Dick had furnished him with funds enough to bear all his expenses, the Club went down to the station to see him started on his way home. A happier or more grateful boy than Chase was that day never lived. The Club often heard of him after that. While they were prosecuting their voyage around the world, he and Wilson were attending the Bellville Academy—the new buildings having been completed by this time,—and they made it a point to keep their friends on board the Stranger posted in all that went on there.

Having seen Chase off, and the Pike and his family settled for the winter in comfortable quarters near the Fort, the Club began active preparations for their journey across the mountains. Old Winter had only just " shown his teeth," so Dick Lewis said. The roads were not yet impassable, but soon would be, and if the journey to San Francisco was to be made that winter, it must be undertaken at once.

So the Club started without delay, Dick and old Bob acting as guides. Of the adventures that befell them at the other end of their journey, we shall have something to say in " FRANK NELSON IN THE FORE-CASTLE ; OR, THE SPORTSMAN'S CLUB AMONG THE WHALERS."

THE END.